DENIS KEHOE was born in Dublin in 1978, where he now lives. He has studied philosophy and European culture, literature and thought. He teaches film studies, media and English. *Walking on Dry Land* follows Denis Kehoe's much praised first novel, *Nights Beneath the Nation*.

Praise for *Nights Beneath the Nation*

'Kehoe writes this engaging tale of long-buried secrets with poetic flair' *Gay Times*

'Vivid… a bold and confident debut… This heartfelt tale of love, loss and the possibilities of redemption marks out Denis Kehoe to be a very promising writer indeed' *Attitude*

'This is a remarkable, sharply observed and engaging book which deserves to be well received. Although most of the central characters are gay it is not a gay novel, nor indeed even a book about being gay; it is a book about being alive and being human in Ireland from the 1950s to the present day… the very period is caught in an extraordinary feat of creative memory… Part mystery, part love story, this remarkable first novel has for me echoes of that wonderful Spanish novel *Shadow of the Wind*. I lived through most of the period described in this book and I can attest to its authenticity –

Walking on Dry Land

DENIS KEHOE

A complete catalogue record for this book can be obtained from the
British Library on request

First published in 2011 by Serpent's Tail,
an imprint of Profile Books Ltd
3A Exmouth House
Pine Street
London EC1R 0JH
www.serpentstail.com

ISBN 978 1 84668 781 5
eISBN 987 1 84765 659 9

Designed and typeset by sue@lambledesign.demon.co.uk

Printed and bound in Britain by Clays, Bungay, Suffolk

10 9 8 7 6 5 4 3 2 1

Mixed Sources
Product group from well-managed
forests and other controlled sources
www.fsc.org Cert no. TT-COC-002227
© 1996 Forest Stewardship Council

The paper this book is printed on is certified by
the © 1996 Forest Stewardship Council A.C. (FSC).
It is ancient-forest friendly. The printer holds
FSC chain of custody SGS-COC-2061

For my good friend Adriana and my sister Susan

'I think what creates in me the deep sense I have of living out of step with others is the fact that most people think with their feelings whereas I feel with my thoughts'

Fernando Pessoa, *The Disquiet of Being*

Tenho saudades da minha mãe,
Quando penso nela, começo a chorar.
Ficarei assim, ficarei assim,
Ai ai, a minha mãe.

I miss my mother,
When I think of her, I start to cry.
I will stay like this, I will stay like this,
Ai, ai, my mother.

Song sung by soldiers during the civil war in Angola

'But the camera sees with its own eye. It sees things the human eye does not detect'

Douglas Sirk

'For me, texts are death, images are life… We need both: I am not against death'

Jean-Luc Godard

1

Lisbon: December 2006

ANA LEFT THE HOTEL and walked out onto Avenida da Liberdade. A silent, foggy night: hushed, darkened beneath the elegant Christmas lights. Empty save for the occasional couple walking home with their *Bolo Rei* in its illustrated cardboard box, tied up with ribbon, held in gloved hands. And the homeless, making their beds in the doorways of grand buildings, or wandering up and down: junkies, men freefalling into old age and the girl with the big eyes who looked like she belonged in an ad or music video, not dying slowly out here on these streets.

It had been a long day and Ana was hungry, tired. The TAP plane hadn't arrived in Dublin that morning, simply hadn't turned up, so she'd had to come through Heathrow. Standing for hours behind middle-aged couples off skiing for the holidays, noticing enormous Bangladeshi clans and listening to an Italian girl arguing with an airport worker about how many bags she could take on board with her.

Ana caught sight of her reflection in the glass façade of a building further along, smoothed out an eyebrow and quickly redid her lipstick. Before she turned and noticed the light coming from a restaurant that reminded her of a train, on one of the concrete islands that ran the length of the avenue.

'Good evening! Is the kitchen still open?' she asked the lone waiter, who seemed ready to pull into the last station of life himself. He took an exaggerated, myopic look at his wrist-watch before he motioned her to a table. Grudging should be a byword for the Portuguese, she thought to herself. No charm, no affability, weight of the world on their shoulders. But enough! She wouldn't be drawn in, refused to become embroiled in this game of silly, silent recriminations.

The seafood rice arrived soon after she'd ordered it, hot, nourishing, wet. And eating it quickly, hungrily, Ana looked out at this silent city at the end of the world and began to imagine herself as a spy who had slipped in over the waves and would disappear the next morning without anybody knowing she'd been here. Sleeping in an art nouveau hotel, the statues of two gold boys standing sentinel at the foot of the stairs, gliding along these streets and watching every footfall from within this glass box. It felt illicit, delicious.

Because the truth was this was her home, Lisbon. Was where she'd grown up, in any case. Not here in the centre of town, with its uphill, downhill, sardine-smelling, fado-whining, crumbling old *bairros* but out in Carcavelos. Big houses, a long beach, St Julian's private English school where Helena had taught and which she had attended.

That smart suburb where she should have been now, spending the night with her father, whose skin had softened and whose workload had lightened lately. Who was all alone now and even sorry for his sins some days. Daddy!

But she couldn't have handled the trek out to the family apartment: the lying, the not crying. He'd only put his arms around her if she went to see him, wrap her up in his embrace, call her *querida*, make her dinner, coffee, cut up a cake. Apple of his eye, Ana. And that was why she wouldn't go, because she loved him despite everything, loved him fiercely, and didn't have the audacity to lie to him and say she was just going to Angola for a holiday, to spend some time with her brother Tiago. Who had spent the first years of his life in the country and had been back there six already, working as an engineer.

Because what she wouldn't be telling her father was, I'm going to Luanda to find my mother, real mother, biological mother. You know, the woman you slept with behind Helena's back, you Lothario of Luanda, you old devil you! The one who pushed me out nine months after you writhed with her and then handed me over. I'm leaving in the morning to search her out and ask her, face to face, one woman to another, exactly what happened, why I ended up here and not there.

Ana paid the bill and, as she was leaving the restaurant, warmed up by the food and the wine, she felt the urge to go for a walk. Saw herself strolling all the way through the Baixa to Praça do Comércio. Along Rua Augusta, past McDonalds, Zara and Louis Vuitton, down the shiny white cobbled street. Through memories of sunny afternoons and tourists moving slowly, backpacks on lobster-sunburned shoulders, with real artists painting, and con-artists fabricating, then hawking, their pictures and postcards of yellow trams and old churches.

Yes, she felt decisive, picturing the river through the arch that leads into the square, that's what she'd do. Go and take a look at the enormous metal Christmas tree in the *praça*. Stand on the damp stones, faded yellow buildings all around, with the fog coming in off the water. Just to mark the season in the city.

Lisbon: October 1965

A FRIDAY MORNING, a Miles Davis tune, the cobble-stones of Restauradores slick with rain. José de Castro is determined not to slip and fall on his backside, making a fool of himself in front of the early-morning shoppers. He picks his footfall carefully, can afford to move slowly, because he doesn't have any lectures until this afternoon, the hours before then his to do with as he likes. Could while them away in bookshops, sit in smoky old cafés and talk in code with friends about how to start a revolution in Portugal. Or maybe visit an art gallery, buy a new LP.

He walks past Rossio train station and into Rua 1° de Dezembro, lazily contemplating going to Café Nicola for a coffee, then catching sight of the barber in his shop on the other side of the street. No customers in there yet, just the old man carefully reading his newspaper and a long row of leather chairs, empty. José runs a hand through his hair and thinks he might as well use this opportunity to get a trim.

'Good morning,' says the barber as he walks in. And sitting down, as white gown is whipped over him, José catches sight of himself, thinks he doesn't look too bad for twenty-two: hazel eyes, cheeky grin, brown hair. And his suit: slimline, snazzy, black, trousers lifting at the knee to reveal his pride and joy, slick as a whistle Chelsea boots. So sharp you could cut yourself on them.

While at the same time Helena Fonseca is wandering through Chiado, stepping into shoe shops, bookshops, looking at gloves in the narrow windows of Luvaria Ulisses and thinking she wouldn't mind another pair for this winter. Eyes drawn to her own reflection, to the dark tweed blazer and skirt she is wearing, the white blouse beneath. Smart, yes, well-cut, yes, but too bloody conservative. You look much too serious, she says to herself.

I wish I could be more like Diana Scott, her mind drifts. A little badder, a bit more risqué. It's a couple of months since she and two friends from the student residence went to see *Darling*, gazing at the beautiful, brazen blonde and all her fancy clothes, but the film still haunts Helena. Taunts her with everything she is not. Sometimes she finds herself in the morning, hands on hips, lips pouting, trying to look as devil-may-care as Julie Christie, but always ending up looking more like a schoolteacher than a siren. 'Well that's what I am, aren't I? Or will be.' She shrugs her shoulders.

As José walks up Rua Garrett, pleased with himself, dusting stray hairs from the sleeves of his jacket. He goes into Bertrand, the old bookshop with its endless rooms, through arches and arches, picking up English novels by Iris Murdoch and Graham Greene, thinking he could spend all morning in here. After half an hour he finally pays for the new edition of *Cahiers du Cinéma* and decides he'll have a coffee while reading a few of the articles.

A Brasileira is already busy when Helena walks in, the smell of coffee and the clamour of voices startling her out of her daydream. Most of the marble-topped tables are occupied by students, middle-aged couples and old ladies in heavy, expensive jewellery dragging them towards the grave, but when somebody gets up she heads towards the back, thinking nobody will spot her there.

It's the line of people stretched the length of the glass counter full of pastries – elbows out, hands tilted, coffees knocked back – that José notices when he enters the same place ten minutes later. He scans for a spot to sit down and glances up at the heavy clock at the back of the café. Begins walking towards it, caught behind the slow, lumbering movements of a man old enough to be his father. Trundle, trundle, trundle; big bear of a thing, but only after a few moments does it dawn on José, everything else receding into the background, why this man is moving at such a pace, why he seems to be taking everything in. Because, sure enough, yes, there they are, the heavy black shoes give him away in a flash. He's PIDE, the secret police, looking for somebody to terrorise, a victim to play with this morning.

His eyes fall on a young woman nestled into the corner, sitting at the last row of tables, reading a newspaper. Her hair's dark red and her skin pale, fresh. There's a packet of cigarettes on the table and as she reaches out to take one she glances up, only then noticing the man coming towards her. Flicker of fear in her eyes.

She looks away from the oh-so-curious stare, cursing herself for being stupid enough to read the banned student newspaper in a place as public as this. Her heart is thumping as she flicks a match, steeling herself to remain calm. But just then there's a rapid flash of black before her, bright white teeth and the weight of a hand on hers. '*Tudo bem?*' A kiss on each cheek and the pressure of his fingers above her elbow.

Who are you? What's going on? Why are you doing this? she thinks as he bundles up the newspaper and fires it back along the floor with a flick of the wrist saying, 'Would you like anything? I'm going to have a *café com leite.*' His eyes hold hers, smile as fixed as a Colgate advertisement, and Helena can't help but return the expression. Finds it hard to believe this stranger has done this for her, slipped in like Superman and saved the day. 'I'll have the same,' she responds, as José glances around, looking for a waitress.

'So what do you want to do tonight?' he turns back to her, failing to find anybody to give their order to, aware of the stare the officer is still giving them. He notices the dark flecks within her eyes and wonders at the false intimacy born of this game they're playing. 'Go to the theatre? See if there's anything on in the cinema? A nice meal?' he suggests.

'Perhaps the theatre,' she replies.

'Okay, we can see what's on when we leave,' he smirks, maybe chancing his luck now.

But Helena gives as good as she gets, can match his performance word for word. 'And how is your mother?' she asks.

'Oh, she's tremendous,' he answers after a brief pause, slightly embarrassed. 'Still obsessed with cooking and Perry Como. I don't know which is worse; her food or his music.'

She slaps him gently on the sleeve. 'Now, now, don't talk like that. I'm sure she's at home preparing your lunch right now.'

'That has to be a joke,' he says. 'They could get her a job with the Gestapo. This food will make you talk.'

He laughs to himself then and waits a few moments before muttering, 'Is he still there?'

She looks up and watches the PIDE officer head towards

the door. 'He's leaving, thank God,' she says, José turning to watch as the man stares up and down the street, first this way, then that, before walking off into the damp morning.

2

Luanda: December 2006

NIGHT FELL EARLY IN LUANDA, in Angola. That was the first thing Ana noticed as she stepped from the plane into the already dark evening. That and the heat, which didn't so much hit her as wrap her up in its moist fug, before she went inside and waited to get her passport stamped. Handed her yellow fever card over to the official, if that's what he could be called, the munchkin money-maker. She'd been warned about him, told he pounced on unsuspecting visitors who forgot, or hadn't bothered, to get the vaccine. But she wasn't about to be ripped off as soon as she left the plane, cheated by this place again so casually. So she gave him the little card, unsmiling.

Tiago was waiting for her at the baggage claim, creaking empty belt going round and round, had obviously bribed his way in. He gave her a hug, kissed her on both cheeks and smiled to himself at the linen skirt and crisp blouse she was wearing, her attempt at looking like a forties first-timer in Africa. She wondered if he got the irony of the look, the string of false pearls around her neck, but guessed he probably didn't. Was likely just thinking here was his crazy baby sister, with her long curly hair swept up into a bun, and how odd it was to see her standing here in the airport in Luanda, curious eyes following her around, trying to figure her out.

'How's everything with you?' he asked.

'All good,' she replied, 'but busy, you know. Teaching a lot and I've just finished correcting a tonne of essays. I've started a PhD as well. I could do with more time for that.'

'Oh yeah, what's it about?' he inquired.

'Oh, cinematic representations of women in New York City,' her words petered out as she recalled her brother's interests had never really stretched as far as academia. Besides, she didn't really know what to say about her work, except that she was interested in gender representations created by THE twentieth-century art form of cinema, set in THE twentieth-century city of New York. Identity, fashion, space, modernity... she wondered again if she was just clutching at straws.

'Was the flight okay? Any dancing on it?' Tiago's grin widened as they left the terminal twenty minutes later.

'No,' she answered, 'not today.'

'You were lucky,' he said as they pushed past a crowd of young men, all hustle and bustle: baggage carriers, taxi-drivers, shysters. 'Once I flew here at Christmas and there was a party on board. Couples dancing *kizomba* up and down the aisle, everybody drunk.' He shook his head.

Then bent to give a few dollars to a light-skinned woman begging with her baby in the car park, before pushing Ana's suitcase into the back of the jeep and starting up the motor. 'How's Lisbon? How's Dad?' he asked and she felt the shame course through her body like ink rising through a stick of celery in a schoolroom experiment.

'I didn't see him,' she responded, looking at her brother,

cheeks flushed and tongue clumsy. 'I didn't really have time. I'll spend a few days with him on the way back.' Tiago studied her for a couple of seconds longer than she was comfortable with, before returning his eyes to the road.

And when he did she knew that would probably be the end of it. He was always so careful with his little sister, so used by now to her long silences, her retreats from this world. Sometimes she hated herself for how she made him act or not act, cursed herself for still dominating the dynamic between them, milking invisible wounds. Wished, moments like these, that he wouldn't be so understanding, so careful with her and had an almost perverse longing for him to tell her to get a grip, give her a shake, snap her out of it. But there it was, silence, as the shadows of stray figures scurried across dimly-lit roads.

When they walked into his apartment building Tiago high-fived two young guys. 'This is my sister Ana,' he told them. 'Keep an eye out for her. Ana, this is Paulo and Roberto.'

They kissed her warmly and then Paulo, she thought it was Paulo, asked, 'Have you been to Angola before?'

There was a furtive look between herself and Tiago before she thought what the hell. 'I was born here,' she replied, 'but I haven't been back since I was a year old.'

'Well, welcome home then, sister,' Paulo smiled, before Tiago hoisted her suitcase up to his waist and said they'd have to take the stairs because the lift was broken, had been out of order for years, was full of rubbish people had thrown down into the shaft.

Halfway up the second flight of unlit steps, he paused in the darkness for a moment. 'They live under the stairs,' he said. 'The guys, that's where they live, Paulo and Roberto.'

'But what about the dirt and the rats? Aren't there rats?'

Ana couldn't believe it, but Tiago's shoulders just went up and down.

'I suppose it's better than sleeping out on the streets,' he replied, as if a few rats were the least of anybody's worries in Angola.

On they continued, right up to the top floor and along the neighbours' balcony where wife and husband were busy cooking part of an animal Ana thought she recognised but didn't want to. Through the re-enforced metal gate and onto Tiago's own balcony as he gave her a look and whispered, 'What are they up to now, these crazy Congolese?'

Tiago's wife Cristina appeared as soon as they entered the apartment, the two girls behind her; truly shy or just pretending, Ana couldn't say. They looked tiny, beautiful, washed and shining: Carolina and Belita. And when they were all inside Ana bent to kiss them, feeling a bit awkward, going quickly to get the presents she'd brought for them, hoping to bridge whatever intimacy she couldn't manage with a couple of fancy toys, beautifully wrapped.

Before Cristina showed her around, explained how they'd had to put down a new floor, install a water tank in the yard, stretch pipes the length of the wall outside and basically reconstruct the apartment from scratch. Ana wondered what it had looked like before, so basic now it must really have been a dump. 'But it's home,' Cristina was saying, hint of pride at her own resourcefulness running through her voice. 'At first I hated it here in Angola, wanted to get on the first plane back to Portugal, but I like it now. And the kids, they have a good life.' Ana studied her, wondering if she was telling the truth or just trying to convince herself of something, imagined she would probably be defeated by this place within a week.

It must have been hours afterwards when Ana found herself back on the balcony: smoking, drinking beer, drifting towards midnight with Tiago. Cristina and the kids had gone to bed, and with smoking forbidden indoors, they'd been banished out here, six floors above the city, looking down towards the bay. *Annie Hall*, that's what came into Ana's mind: the scene on the terrace of Annie's small apartment when she and Alvy have a glass of white wine after the tennis match where they've met. Just after her manic drive through Manhattan. It was the awkwardness of those moments that sat glaring at her now; the soon-to-be-lovers small-talking away, feeling like fools. With subtitles telling the audience what they're really thinking.

Ana studied Tiago as he traced his hand across the thick night sky, pointing out different buildings. 'That blue one over at Kinaxixi, that's Cuca,' he said. 'That's Chevron, the shiny one, and there's Sonangol. You know, the oil company,' he went on. Talking, talking, as if he was afraid of silence now. 'Things have really changed here since Savimbi was killed,' he turned to her, Ana remembering the story of the rebel UNITA leader finally defeated in the jungle nearly five years before. 'Just look at all the cranes. There are Chinese everywhere, throwing up buildings. And the planes are full of Portuguese coming in every day.'

'Is that right?' she asked, imagining hordes of her countrymen fleeing the flaking city of Lisbon which seemed so bent and broken lately. Down on one knee, with widows in black who had always survived now asking for change outside Cais do Sodré station.

'Yes, yes,' he replied before rambling on, leaving Ana to wonder when they would talk about things that were important. About Helena dying and how Tiago still couldn't accept, not really, not fully, that his mother would never again be found on spring mornings, nursing blossoms on the balcony of their apartment in Carcavelos. That the breast cancer had come back, really come back, and this time eaten her whole. And she asked herself if he'd even mention Conor, probe as to why she'd left the life they were building together, walked away from another man. Or question why she was really here, why exactly she'd come. Ask if she was looking for her, finally trying to find Solange.

In sudden, clear dawnings she felt the reality of being in Angola and the weight of having to do what she'd been putting off for years. That pledge she'd made to herself time and again, getting only as far as fruitless Internet searches before she let her resolve drift away in work, life, living. But now she was really here in Luanda, high above the city, and her back was against the wall. Before long she'd have to begin the search for the woman who had given birth to her. To ask her, if she was still alive, her version of what happened, and make her face the fact that she, Ana, really existed.

And sooner or later she'd have to tell Tiago what she was up to, though she couldn't just blurt that all out now. It sounded so ridiculous, like something from a TV movie, *In Search of My Mother*. And there was the terror of hurting him, the guilt, the betrayal of their family at the heart of her quest. Mother, mother, motherless. Sweat of her palms, the thought that Tiago had never let her down and the memory of a morning long past.

Walking to the park from the shops in Carcavelos, Tiago was about ten, which would have made Ana almost four. And summer, July or August wasn't it? Had to be because neither of them was in school, the trees casting long, shifting shadows along the pavements. And they were dawdling, strolling slowly up Rua Sacadura Cabral; Tiago blowing bubbles with his gum, Ana behind him with her ice-cream dripping all over her hands, when she noticed he'd stopped and was staring across the street at something.

It was the café, the café their father always took them to on Saturday morning for a juice and a *pastel de nata*, but she couldn't understand why he was looking over there, why his face had turned red, the way it did when he got angry and was ready to really explode. So she followed his eyes and it was only then she saw them, sitting on the terrace. Senhora Vieira and Senhora Bento; the spinster and the widow who lived in the same apartment building as Ana and Tiago and were known to meet up every morning to gossip about their neighbours. To drag them down, down, down, and boast to one another about who they had pushed around lately.

But it took Ana a few more moments to figure out that the two sets of dry, hungry eyes were trained directly on her, that they had been following her. And to understand the words they were swapping were careless scissors set to snip her apart, two dogs barking at her heels. Yes, all of a sudden she was coldly certain these two women were busy trading versions of where she came from. Of who she really belonged to, for as sure as they were the guardians of order and respectability in Carcavelos, this child, almost white but not quite, was not the offspring of José and Helena de Castro. There was a story here, a scandal here, and they were so busy inventing their own versions of it, they didn't expect the voice shouting at them from the other side of the street.

'Senhoras, *calem a boca!* Close your mouths! Close your mouths or the flies will get in. The flies will get in!'

Peering out from over their big, out-of-fashion sun-glasses, from beneath their helmet haircuts, they couldn't believe their eyes. There was that little scut, Tiago de Castro, telling them to shut up. And now his little sister was by his side, sticking her tongue out at them and mocking them with a dance she'd learned God knows where. 'Close your mouths, ladies. Close your mouths or the flies will get in,' they shouted in unison a few more times before they ran, laughing, up the street.

Ana looked over at Tiago on the balcony now; tanned, jovial, more at home in this country than she could ever be, perhaps than she would ever want to be. And thought of how close they had once been, wondering if they had grown apart, and whether she had somehow abandoned him when she moved to Dublin and away from all those miles of lies, telling herself not to listen any longer because there were so many versions of the truth. And if there was a distance between them now then she asked if it was her fault. Or José's, or Helena's. Or if the blame could be laid at the feet of those like Senhora Vieira and Senhora Bento, who maybe had won in the end. But perhaps it goes back further than that, she thought, all the way back to Solange and that origi-nal sin. Solange, who might still be somewhere down in that city, silent, smiling angel of destruction.

Lisbon: January 1966

A SATURDAY EVENING at the Cinemateca Portuguesa in its old home at the Palácio Foz. José and Helena have come to watch a film, an Italian film, yes. It's *L'avventura*, *La strada* or *Le notti bianche* with Marcello Mastroianni crying because Jean Marais is finally there at the bridge and Maria Schell has run straight into his big blond arms. Poor Marcello, and it looked as though he really had a chance with her, back when they were dancing in the café.

First time they've seen one another, José and Helena, since she went back to Oporto: cold, stone, misty, green, for Christmas. He takes her hand, wondering why he feels slightly disappointed, been waiting for this so long. Feels her fingers heavy and awkward, then looks at her; beautiful, clever, and tries to let such thoughts drift away.

While she's wondering if this could be something long-term: man of her life, man and wife. Oh, he's no Burt Lancaster or Kirk Douglas; he-man hands around her waist, I'm melting, I'm melting, taking her out of her existence, whisking her off into another way of being. But maybe he's all the better for that. Not like other smiling seducers who've courted her, busy playing a game of submission and control, wanting only to dive into her peach-white skin and take something from her.

She enjoys José; the time they spend together, seeing each other every day almost. With their walks in the Jardim Botânico, their coffees and conversations about new films, old books. Afternoons spent slowly shopping in the Baixa, women with fish piled on their heads and seagulls circling above. That day they walked all the way to Belém, strolling through the Ribeiro market, pausing once and then again by the dockyards for a dangerous, delicious kiss.

And José too, watching a street scene, is now busy asking himself what exactly it is that's between them; what has brought them back together after the Christmas break. Wondering how it is that they've become part of one another's lives. Because they are, aren't they? Each of them is what the other does, is becoming… perhaps.

He thinks of the dinners in cheap *tascas* in Bairro Alto and Alfama, the long walk by the sea at Cascais that bright, cold Sunday afternoon in December, the cake and coffee afterwards. And how his heart soared and prick swelled slowly, exquisitely, dancing with Helena to the jazz in the Hot Clube de Portugal. He glances over at her again, strokes her cheek.

And when the film has finished, he arranges his grey lambswool scarf before they walk out onto Restauradores, heading for a hot chocolate at a nearby café, just another young couple strolling into life.

3

Luanda: December 2006

A NAME AND A PHOTOGRAPH, that was all Ana had. Should have asked for more, made her father and Helena give her some real information, but it was never a topic they encouraged her to speak about, to explore evenings at dinner in Carcavelos. Though it was always there: beside them, beneath them, between them. Only talking about it out loud would have given the beast a name, a voice; saying the unsaid, raising the dead, Mother. And Ana could never be the one to do that: the shame and embarrassment at being a bastard, a big dark secret unspoken, sitting heavy and stupid on her plate.

So instead she grew up quiet, silent, trying not to draw attention to herself. And teenage years were too angry, too raw, to go begging for the truth, to want to put herself together again with facts long suppressed, life long gone, whistling Dixie.

But in silence, in secret she would look for clues some-times. Sporadically, hungrily, Wednesday evenings when she was fourteen, fifteen and there was nobody in the apart-ment: parents gone shopping and Tiago at the swimming pool. Sharp, sly, slinking into their bedroom to look for anything that could give her a way into where she came from, a reason why things had turned out as they had. Because there had to be one, didn't there? Some sense as to why she'd wound up here in Lisbon instead of playing in the dusty streets and sleeping by her mother in Luanda.

Helena's things were what she always started with, making a show of looking through the drawers of her dressing table, in her jewellery box, hands on nylon stockings, silk scarves, ornate brooches, though what she was really interested in was what belonged to her father. That was where the goods were, or might be. Turning the pages of the pile of books by his side of the bed, slipping her fingers into the inside pockets of his blazers. Then opening, slowly, the drawer with his underwear in it, neatly folded when first put in but now just small piles of toppling-over cotton; briefs mostly, moulded to carry his sex, his behind, the odd pair of boxer shorts, pastel-striped.

The burning of her cheeks as she'd take them in her hands, a dryness in her throat as she imagined him lying down with this young woman, putting himself so eagerly into her, deep brown legs apart, his penis straining for her, and the start of a wetness between her own legs.

Usually she didn't discover anything concrete, any information she might use against her father and Helena. It was more that sudden, wild sense of his sin, the scent of animal off him and a vague feeling of complicity. With Helena firmly shut out. Just he and Solange in a humid, darkened hotel room as the city went on outside. And Ana, sitting like a sleepwalker in the bedroom, suddenly part of the infidelity, of the act, of something. Not just the ill-defined mistake to come out of it, blurred around the edges.

But it was one of those Wednesday evenings she actually

found something, after she'd really pulled everything apart, looked frantically through all his things, Daddy Dearest. Anxious, eager, to discover something real now, instead of drifting between here and there; remembering, forgetting, fingers trailing her thigh. She'd put the shoe box with the old payslips back under the bed, then taken the ladder, climbed up the wardrobe, and removed a pile of old magazines on top of it. Wondering, as she flicked their pages, if she was just wasting time again, thinking she would only have to clean all this mess up later, when there it was.

A photograph, 1970s, bright colours faded, like the ones in the leather albums in the lounge, and in it two young women, two good-looking *mulatas*. One was wearing denim flares and a tight yellow top, hair hidden beneath a headscarf, the other with some African material wrapped into a dress around her body. Resting their arms on one another's shoulders, breasts and behinds out, midriffs in, smiling.

Heart thudding, Ana wondered if this was really happening. Listened as she told herself that one of these women could really be her mother and considered if she should keep the photo. After all, there seemed something so familiar in the slightly awkward stance of the girl in the yellow and the way she looked at the camera, bold but self-conscious at the same time. She stared into her eyes until the image became blurred, then noticed the gangly limbs of the other girl, in the fabric, a *pano* it was called, and saw some potential there too.

But probably neither of them is Solange and they have no connection to her, Ana reasoned. Is there really any point in keeping it? She began to doubt herself, suddenly frightened of what she was doing. Perhaps they were just friends of my parents. Or some whores José slept with who gave him a photo as a memento. Other ladies he laid with, who could say?

She was about to leave, put the picture back where she'd found it, let life reform around its previous contours, but then the thought came to her that she might regret it, could need this one day, this possible clue to where she was from. So she took the photograph and photocopied it the following afternoon, before returning it to its grave among the dying pages of the old magazine.

Ana looked at the black and white photocopy in her hand now. It too had faded. Kept for years with family photos, taken out a few early Friday evenings one November when she was tired after the week and held above her head as she lay spread out on her bed. Or pulled out when she got wound up, all set to take control of this story, to find her mother and ask her the truth. Sure this time she'd do it, really do it, not like before when she let it recede to the back of her mind as something she should do. Would do if life weren't so busy teaching, putting classes together, and sitting for hours in the library, turning the pages of books about the male gaze, mind drifting to memories of Helena talking about the Sweater girls of the 1950s.

She was alone in the apartment, Tiago at work and Cristina out with the girls, so she could make the call she'd been putting off since she arrived. Telling herself she needed a few days to get used to the city, to acclimatise, to spend time with Tiago and his family before she began the search. Started something she was now reluctant to begin, sitting in the middle of the morning silence.

But she had to ring Lena, Mariana's mother, to ask her if she'd ever known either of the young women in the photograph. If she'd come across a Solange Mendes back before independence, in the years before the civil war. Because Mariana had told Ana her mother knew everybody in Luanda, from ministers in the government to women selling fruit in Roque Santeiro market. She'd been born in Luanda, spent her life there, sending Mariana and her sister to school in Lisbon only when things were looking really bad.

And who knew, perhaps she'd even lead her straight to Solange. Or tell her it was no use, that she was long gone; hit by a stray bullet, a victim of malaria, poverty or neglect. There were moments when Ana wasn't sure which would be better, to find her living or dead.

Her mind drifted to that night with Mariana in London, back in October. The Cuban restaurant in Islington and Megan's glances at a good-looking girl sitting at a table on her own. Trying to make Mariana jealous; the angry lips, sulky posture, movement of her eyes from one of the women to the other to the other. But maybe she isn't to blame, Ana had thought at the time, Mariana probably stirred things up a bit before they left their flat.

'My friend Ana's in town. I'm gonna meet her for dinner tomorrow night. Wanna come?' she could hear Mariana.

'Who's Ana?' the slow reply, disinterest feigned.

'Oh, just an old friend.' Or, 'Just an old flame from secondary school.' Maybe, 'My cute little *Angolana*, the one with the curly hair.' That would be Mariana all right. Making something out of nothing much, calculating a bit of drama, a bit of spice to lace the night with.

Even if it was true there had been a bit of an affair, if that's what it could be called, back when Mariana swaggered into St Julian's from Angola, like some creature that had swum up the ocean, crawled along the beach and walked straight into the posh English school. Looking down her nose at the place from the get-go. Even the teachers had been intimidated by Mariana. Not physically; she was tall, yes, but not of a heavy build. It wasn't that, but her combination of attitude and intelligence that set them slightly shivering.

'Here, let me give you my mother's number,' she'd said that night in Islington. 'She'll help you no problem. Will be glad to meet a friend of mine. She might be busy coming up to Christmas but give her a call. I'm sure she'll meet you for dinner or something.'

'Does she still like it over there?' Ana had wondered, picturing Luanda already.

'Yeah, she does,' Mariana replied. 'Could never live outside Africa. It's in her, you know, in her down to her feet. Two months in Lisbon and she's running back there. Says they have no sense of humour, the Portuguese, that they're so small-minded and she can feel the life being sucked out of her.'

'Would you two ever go and live there?' Ana tried to draw Megan into the conversation, drag her away from the silly game she was playing that was really only amusing herself. Megan looked like living in Angola was the last thing that would cross her mind, staring at Ana as if she was crazy, asking if she'd walk away from London for some shithole in the arse-end of Africa.

'I don't know,' it was Mariana who answered, 'I still miss the sunshine. And the food. Look at my skin, I'm practically grey here.' She showed Ana a wrist that didn't shine milk-chocolate brown the way it had on the beach that summer just after they'd finished secondary school. 'The men are a

bit of a pain though. God's gift, the lot of them. Tsk. Fools!'
There was a throaty laugh. 'The girls aren't bad though.'

It was that night, Ana kept recalling now, when she
should have just been phoning Lena. The half a pineapple
full of rice and prawns, Mariana's warm eyes and Megan
seething and silent until a couple of glasses of wine had taken
the chill out of her. Before they went off in search of whatever fun was to be found on a Sunday night in London.

Mariana, first girl Ana had ever kissed. First *person* she'd
ever kissed for that matter. And in the end it was she who'd
made the first move, braiding Mariana's hair in her auntie's house in Parede, the woman singing and watering the
plants downstairs, Ana's breath steady behind her friend
on the bed, fingers long and nimble, unsure of her feelings
but certain they were there. And Mariana, with her nipples
pressed against her blouse, head trusting in her hands.

Nobody had said anything smart to Ana since Mariana
showed up at the school. Spineless bitches skitter-scattered
when they saw them coming now: Mariana, Ana and Linda.
Linda who had always been around but who Ana had been
ashamed to speak to, in case it made her stand out even
more. Because Linda was the darkest girl in the school, skin
the colour of the Coca-Cola she rubbed on it summer days
to make it shine.

And as Ana ran her fingers along her friend's neck, all
she could think was that she was surprised this hadn't happened before. Only then she noticed that Mariana's heart
was slamming against her chest, that her body had started
shaking, and she understood suddenly it was her friend
who had been waiting for her to make the first move all this
while. Mariana with the big mouth and all that sass, Ana
could see now how frightened she was of her desires, of her

dreams at night, the longing between her legs for the touch of a breast, a belly, a beauty.

She put one hand on her friend's shoulder, lifted her chin with the fingers of her other hand, before taking her fleshy, hungry lips in her own.

Lisbon: April 1966

THERE HAD TO BE MORNINGS like these, didn't there? Her lips painted, hair down and smelling of camomile shampoo, tiny feet in sandals she can only walk in very slowly because they cut into her heels. His navy slacks, cashmere sweater and white shirt that brings out his early tan. All set off by two-tone leather shoes that click as they hit the street. And the sunglasses he saw in a French film, later bought in a shop in the Baixa.

It's a Saturday as he sets out from his parents' apartment in Campo de Ourique, thinking he might as well walk; it's a nice morning. Feeling his heart stirring, moving, lifting, as he passes the Jardim da Estrela because he's going to meet Helena. Nearly two weeks now since he saw her last, since she went home to Oporto for the Easter holidays. And that strange feeling of relief when he left her at Santa Apolónia train station. Before watching a homeless old woman drinking from a street fountain, suddenly aware of all the time he'd have alone.

But all he wants this morning in April is to see her, to laugh with her, kiss her, take her for lunch and let the day unfold drowsily, maybe finishing up in the cinema or at dinner, perhaps a party at a friend's house. So sure of Helena today, so sure they'll make the grade.

Half an hour later and he's in front of Café Nicola. He stands for a moment at the door before entering, seeing Helena already there, her hair and the blouse she's wearing set off by the smoky grey and silver art deco fixtures. Sitting, reading a book, beneath an old painting of a couple out for a stroll, the woman in a long dress and a fluffy white wig, holding her companion's arm. He takes off his sunglasses, hips languid as he moves up to her.

'Good morning Ms Fonseca,' he grins at her. She looks up and smiles. Notices that he seems taken by surprise. Guesses it's probably because she looks good today, knows these clothes suit her, and that two weeks of a mother's cooking, of being back in the bosom of her family, can do wonders for a girl.

'How was the trip? How are your family?' José asks, looking as though he wants to fall straight into her.

'Good,' she replies. 'My father had a few days off during Easter week so we visited Santiago.'

'Don't tell me you went on some kind of a pilgrimage?' he teases.

'Not exactly,' she laughs, 'but it was nice for my mother. And I enjoyed the visit. It's a beautiful place.'

'Well, once you don't join the nuns or anything like that.'

'You never know, they might still have me,' she responds.

'Not if I have anything to do with it, they won't,' he chuckles, and she can see the desire in his eyes this bright morning, can feel the electricity between them.

Is reassured by his obvious interest because there are times when he runs hot and cold, seems to be living in another time zone where everything is put obsessively through the rational mill of his mind. When he is consumed by incessant analysis, silent sojourns into his own world, own words running through his head. José, so caught up in himself, so full of himself, epicentre of the universe. As if his thoughts, his feelings, the fall of his hair, cut of his cloth were the most urgent, imperative things in life. At times she wants to shake him, drag him out into reality. But she could never do that to him; silly, sad José busy being a man.

Besides, this morning he's handsome and seems wild about her. Looks like he could make swift, amazing love to her, hold her in his grip for hours. And she might make love right back to him, lie naked with him for the afternoon, if only she could be sure they were really going somewhere, that she wasn't just wasting her time with him. It's not that she doesn't want to go all the way, that she hasn't thought about it; more that, sitting here, looking like she does on a day like today, is probably her trump card, the last one she'll turn over when he puts his on the table. If he doesn't turn out to be the joker in the pack, that is, wasting six months of her life already.

'How was Easter here?' she asks him.

'Oh, fine, I had a lot of reading to catch up on but I got to the beach for a swim twice.'

'Was the water cold?' she asks.

'A little,' he replies. 'But you know me anyway, Man of Steel,' and he flexes his muscles like an actor from a silent film. Making her curl up in laughter at his exaggerated pose, the serious, superficial look on his face and the thought of skinny José as some kind of a muscle man.

'Watch out, Johnny Weissmuller,' she says, before he begins to laugh too.

4

Luanda: December 2006

A VAGUE IMAGE OF AN OLD HOUSE in Havana, then a Carcavelos street. That's what passed through Ana as she waited outside Lena's home. The sense, the thought, that these streets and the old houses that lined them were like a mixture of the two places – somewhere between the crumbling mansions of the Cuban capital and the free-standing art deco houses in the area where she'd grown up. Which she'd learned to appreciate, architecture-wise, as an adult, but had only ever wanted to leave, back then. As she lifted her hand to rap on the metal gate, she glanced back at the road, thinking even the epicentre of Castro's idea of paradise didn't have sewers running alongside the city's streets, open drains next to the deformed sidewalks.

'Who is it?' a deep, harassed voice, just audible over the loud barking of a dog on the other side.

'It's Ana,' she steeled herself, falling into her ghetto stance, disposing of the vulnerable, the gentle, hair in two long plaits, wearing her *Jaws* T-shirt and a pair of tailored navy shorts. There was a sound of fingers on metal and the next moment she was staring into canine jowls dripping in saliva, heavy paws on her chest.

'Get out of here! Get out of here!' Lena shouted, dragging the dog away by the collar and giving Ana, slightly irritated but otherwise unruffled, just enough time to pet Gino's rump and get a good look at his owner.

'She's butcher than her lesbian daughter,' was what she thought, taking in Lena's short hair and well-packed build, a circus show in a brightly-striped kaftan. She caught herself then and wondered why this sudden, unnecessary antagonism. After all, Lena had agreed to help her. Had invited her to her house that same afternoon, unhesitatingly, so they could have a decent chat and see what all this was about. Perhaps that was why though. Because she'd put her on the spot, leaving Ana no real option but to agree to the spontaneous meeting, forcing her to make up some silly excuse to Cristina about visiting a friend of a friend. Refusing a lift, saying the woman only lived a few streets away, she knew how to get there, and it couldn't be that dangerous to walk the short distance alone. That she'd see them later for dinner.

And here she was, resentment rising in her stomach, wanting to turn and leave because she wasn't ready for this. Needed more time, a little space alone, to get her head around what she'd started. To compose a few questions to ask this woman, create a face that wouldn't make her seem like some loser come searching for a life, an unrealistic link with an imagined past. But instead she'd been whisked out of her way-it-should-have-been, way-the-story-is-supposed-to-go, in a flash. Hadn't even got as far as suggesting another date because Lena had done all the talking, said she was going to Mussulo in the morning for Christmas and wouldn't be back until New Year's Eve. 'Come around and see me later on today,' she'd commanded. 'I'll see what I can do. Ok, sweetheart?' 'Ok,' Ana had agreed, intimidated into accepting, bowels beginning to echo, yearning for a cigarette.

She followed Lena into the house, slightly taken aback when the woman gripped her in a bear hug and planted two kisses on her cheeks as soon as she'd closed the door. 'Ana, a pleasure to meet you. Sorry about the dog.' She lit a cigarette. 'So, how's my crazy daughter? Have you seen her recently?' the question was casually put as Ana looked around the sitting room; the bright white walls with paintings of African scenes; swathes of greens, oranges and pinks.

'She's good,' came the distracted reply. 'I had an email from her last week. She said she's going to Brazil for Christmas. I suppose she's there now.'

'She arrives today. Lucky her, eh?' Lena smiled. 'And how's Megan? Is Mariana treating her well? Are they getting on okay?'

Ana felt an awkwardness in her hands, being asked like this to dissect her friend's relationship. 'They seem to be doing fine,' she answered, wondering what Mariana had told her mother about their own time together, how they'd lain on the bed in Lena's sister's house, holding one another whole afternoons.

'What will you have to drink? Gin, whisky, wine, juice, coffee? Me, I'm going to have a gin and tonic.'

Ana considered for a moment. 'I'll join you,' she replied, thinking the alcohol might take the edge off things.

'Ó Maria, Maria,' Lena called, and in came a woman about Ana's age; dark skin and mischievous eyes, holding a shirt in her hand, obviously in the middle of ironing. A hello to Ana and a big bright smile before Lena asked her to bring them their drinks.

'Okay, just a minute,' she smiled again and walked off.

'So tell me, Ana, tell me how I can help?' Lena dropped her voice, leaning forward, legs apart, elbows on knees. Sitting on an armchair perpendicular to the battered, brown leather sofa Ana had settled on, one she wouldn't have minded for her own rented place. Which somehow didn't seem real now, that small ex-Corporation house in The Tenters, sitting in the grey-white light and stillness of a Dublin winter. She saw the Huguenots stretching out their linen on tenterhooks, to be bleached by the sun. And hoped for a brief moment Lenny wouldn't leave a cigarette burning all night or bring some dodgy one-night stand back, some prick who'd leave him with a big grin on his face and the house with everything of value under his arm.

'Well, it's like this,' Ana began, snapping out of it, focusing on Lena again, meeting the woman's eye and thinking how impossible this would have been for her to say once, 'I'm looking for my mother.' A breath. 'Her name is Solange Mendes and as far as I know she is a singer. Or *was* a singer, at least. Here, I think one of these girls might be her.' She handed the tatty photocopy to Lena, who put on a pair of smart, dark brown glasses.

As she looked at the image, Ana glanced around the room again, taking in the Mia Couto novel open on the table and the small pile of books on a chair by the door. Lena squinted one last time. 'No, I don't think I know either of them, but the photo was taken a long time ago, wasn't it?' she said.

'Yes, and this photocopy isn't in the best of shape,' Ana replied.

'A bit like me,' Lena laughed throatily and gave the picture back. 'Now where is that drink? Ó Maria,' she called above singing coming from the kitchen. 'Are you awake today?'

'I'll be there now,' Maria chimed back as Lena shook her head and got up to see just what was going on.

'This girl will be the death of me. Ó Maria!' she pleaded and went to the kitchen, leaving Ana wondering if that was it, was all the time she got in terms of her mother. Hating Lena, despising her fat, indifferent ass wading off to the kitchen.

I could always just get up and leave, the bitter temptation began to rise inside her, when her host and Maria came in with the drinks on a tray. 'Cigarette?' Lena offered as she sat back down.

'Thanks,' Ana took the drink from Maria and a cigarette from Lena, held it up for her to light, noticing the rings beneath her eyes, much darker than the rest of her slack, sallow skin.

'Merry Christmas,' Lena cheered, clinking her glass against Ana's, then sitting back into her chair. 'Oh, that's good,' she shook her head, laughing out loud, Ana thinking, yes, it was good, this rush of alcohol.

'So your parents lived here before, did they, Ana?' Lena asked, taking a long look at her, blatant as can be.

'Yes, for ten years.'

'Oh yeah? What's your father's name?'

'José, José de Castro.'

'Zé?' Lena looked at her grinning. 'Worked for a publisher, lived down by the Marginal?'

'Yes, he did work for a publisher here. Did you know him?' Ana asked.

'Dark hair, slim, always dressed well?' Lena looked for confirmation.

'That sounds like him all right,' Ana replied, remembering old photographs she'd seen of her father back in his Alain Delon days.

'Of course I knew him. Everybody in Luanda knew José. Such a nice guy. How is he?'

'He's good,' Ana responded.

'And Helena, how is Helena?' Lena ploughed on, then caught the confused look that flickered across Ana's face as soon as the question came out of her mouth. 'It is Helena, isn't it? José's wife?' she queried, voice falling with each syllable uttered.

'She died earlier this year,' Ana replied, looking down at the floor, thinking of Helena so small against the big white pillows of the hospital bed.

'Oh, I'm sorry to hear that, sweetheart,' Lena offered her condolences.

'It's okay,' Ana answered. 'Breast cancer, you know. It came back again and again.' Lena nodded her head, in a way that told Ana she *did* know, knew exactly what she meant, but her own mind was drifting elsewhere. To that morning in Lisbon the summer just gone and walking in the Jardim Botânico, cracked earth, old leaves, the whole place slouching towards a final drought. With a litter of abandoned kittens living in a bin by the rusted back gate. The pointlessness of it all; the emptiness of the day, the city, her heart, that was the feeling that had gripped her as she flopped down onto a bench in the shade of an old tree. Just before the sudden, tired tears and the calm certainty that Helena was gone, that it was time to find Solange.

She took a long draught of her gin and tonic. 'So you've no idea how I can find Solange?' she managed after a silence that stretched itself out into the four corners of the white room.

Lena smiled doubtfully. 'Let me have a think. Solange. Solange,' she repeated. 'Solange is a common name, you know, sweetheart. Mendes too. But you said she was a singer, no?'

'Yes, as far as I know. Back in '74, '75 anyway.'

'Hmmm, that doesn't make it any easier. Half the people in Luanda were singers back then. This place was really swinging, let me tell you.'

'Oh yeah?' Ana probed, knowing they were moving away from the real point of the conversation, but enjoying it.

'Eeeeh,' Lena was emphatic, 'the whole city was jiving then, in the sixties and seventies. Down in Maxinde, Giro-Giro, Salão dos Anjos. Everybody together: blacks, whites, you name it. It was fantastic.' Ana gazed at her; interest sparked, magic lantern slides of the past flickering to life in the room. Lena obviously caught on that she had sparked her guest's interest. She gave her another cigarette, took one herself, and lit them both up.

'This place was really different back then, Ana, you know, before the civil war. Much safer, much friendlier. Not like today. Half the city living like it's in prison, other half without a pair of shoes to its name. Ha!' she slapped her leg as Ana gazed at her, wide-eyed. 'Used to be something, have something, you know! Most beautiful city south of the Sahara. And look at it now. It's in ruins, chaos. You can't even walk to the shop without someone hassling you. And the government, don't get me started. Twenty-five years of war and look at the state of the place.' She lifted her hand in the direction of the window and the tumult of the city outside, before she took a deep breath. 'Another drink?' she proposed, lifting up the blue bottle of gin.

'Yes please,' Ana said. Before she took her chance. 'Do you think there's any way you could have seen Solange back then, singing in one of the clubs?'

Lena raised her hands, as if in vain. 'It's possible, but, like I say, there were a hell of a lot of singers around. You don't know what clubs she sang in or anything about her band?' Ana shook her head regretfully. 'Okay, don't worry,' Lena had an idea. 'I know a woman singer. She's quite famous here in Angola, been around forever. Maybe she knew Solange, maybe she can help you. I'll give her a call.' And before Ana could protest, get her head around another meeting, Lena was up and dialling her friend's number.

'Ó Luísa, it's me, Lena,' she near-shouted into the mobile. 'Good, good. Listen, I have a girl here, a friend of Mariana's, and she's looking for her mother.' Ana felt her cheeks start to glow, slapped by the bluntness of the words. 'Yes. Her name was Solange Mendes. Solange *Mendes*.' Lena looked at Ana and shook her head disparagingly. 'Yes, that's the one. Solange Mendes. Okay. No, it was just an idea. At your place, then. When, when? Next week. Okay, okay, okay, I'll give her your number. Thanks. *Tchau. Beijos.*'

Lena scrawled the number on a scrap of paper and handed it to Ana. 'Here, this is the woman I was telling you about, Luísa. She says she'd be happy to meet you, lives up in Bairro Operário.' Ana felt a small wave of possibility in her stomach, followed by the gnawing thought that she could hardly head off to this woman's house on her own, walk right the way across the city. Of course she could always ask Tiago to drive her and pretend she was just going to see some friend from home, but that would only mean more lies, more searching for something she couldn't share with her brother, a life that was hers alone.

Maybe it's a bad idea, she began to convince herself. And perhaps this woman won't be any help at all, just another dead end, a lousy red herring. She smiled at the detective jargon racing through her brain. And how she'd always fancied herself as the femme fatale of a film noir but had somehow ended up the detective now: hard-boiled, Philip Marlowe style, out to solve this mystery of her genesis, to track down the real lethal woman. Beaten to the juiciest of roles by Solange.

'Okay, I'll give her a call. Thanks for contacting her,' Ana said.

'It's nothing darling,' Lena looked at her. 'Now let's have another drink,' she proposed as the electricity thudded to a halt, everything deathly silent before the generator slowly chugged to life. Lena sighed, exasperated, before she stretched a single word lengthily to its last syllable; 'An-go-la.'

Lisbon: June 1966

PERHAPS IT WOULD BE NICE, living somewhere else for a while, Helena thinks, sitting below the Castelo de São Jorge. Going to London or Paris now that her exams have finished; Mick and Marianne, beautiful children of the revolution, Jean Seberg walking the length of the Champs-Elysées, '*New York Herald Tribune. New York Herald Tribune.*' Why not leave Lisbon for a few years? she considers. Shake a bit of the dust off, go somewhere the whole world isn't watching everything you do. Especially if he's going to say what she thinks he is.

He's late again, José, always chasing himself, thinking he has all the time in the world, then feeling his heart sink and his lower back quiver because it's going to turn out the way it always does; him nearly making it but not quite, arriving five or ten minutes after the appointed time. He notices a woman in her sixties; soft brown eyes, grey hair, face of a girl, looking out the open window of the tram; watches her watching the city as it moves past. Looking at the walls of buildings nearly close enough to touch, wondering at the magic of these cobbled hills even though she's travelled up and down them the length of her life. He asks himself if he'll miss these things.

'I'll end it, put an end to it before he has a chance to,' Helena thinks to herself as the waiter walks off to bring her a coffee, as she looks out at the rooftops and the expanse of river in the evening light. 'I'm sick of him, of this, anyway. Maybe it's time we went our own ways. Lifted ourselves from this seabed we've settled on and began to live, really live, again.'

She hasn't enjoyed the occasions they've met this past month, his narks, his irritations. Though there haven't been that many, since they were both doing exams. And during those weeks he seems, somehow, to have drifted into the background. She can't explain, can't entirely understand it, but his presence in her life, her mind, his beginning to be a part of who she is, has faded. Other things have taken over, chats with the girls from the residence, a night out at the pictures with one of them, and everybody relating their plans for the future. Other possibilities? she wonders. More to life than low-yield love in Lisbon?

He wants her to come, come with him. Or thinks he does, thinks he should. Wants to do the right thing by her anyway. But it isn't just that, their story is bigger, more complex. He can't see himself going without her; that much is true at least. And the thought of leaving her here is too much for him to bear. Makes his heart creak along with the old wood of the tram, the woman's eyes still fixed on the next curve of the track.

He remembers how he would probably be getting shipped out to the colonial wars with all the others, now that he has finished university, if it weren't for the tuberculosis, the disastrous medical. Feels lucky, relieved, then experiences a twist of shame before he moves away from it. But what if things don't turn out the way they should? his mind turns back to Helena. What if she isn't the one for me? The possibility of a terrible failure seems to grow stronger as the tram grinds to a halt, a cold shiver running through him.

Oh, maybe I'm wrong. Perhaps I've got it all confused, she ponders, suddenly doubting her ability to read the signs of love's progression. She wonders if she's being too hasty. It's not like her, usually so considered, so careful, listening to both sides of the story before making up her mind about anything. What if I regret this? And it's just pride whispering in my ear, playground fears of having my heart broken here on this hill? She decides she'll allow him to speak, give him a little time at least.

And if he does put love's young dream to death this evening, then it won't be the end of the world, the termination of life as she knows it. She'll simply walk off into the evening breeze, down into the Baixa and up Rua Augusta, stroll all the way to the student residence which she's leaving next week anyway. And by the time she reaches the heavy wooden door she'll have a plan. She'll know what to do. She straightens up in her chair.

And her back is to him as he moves towards her, his head spinning and thoughts forgotten in the rush, the rash, to take the leap, to get on with it, get it over with. He runs his fingers lightly over her shoulder before he takes the chair opposite. Catches the confidence of her posture and wonders why she needs him, if indeed she does. Then feels the sudden jolt of the possibility that she might say no as he looks into her eyes. Realises she could tell him she is happy here. Wish him all the best and send him on his way because she knows she'll be fine, is sure of finding somebody else interested in her charms, as sure as she was of passing her exams.

A spoon clatters to the ground and as he bends to retrieve it, he notices the sweat of his armpits, feels the whole city silent, expectant, waiting for him to speak. Oh God, he thinks, and out it comes. 'My uncle Vicente has asked me to go to Angola. He has a job for me at the publisher.' Helena is silent, gaze steady, ready. 'I wanted to know if you'd come with me. Come and live in Angola,' he begins to smile, despite himself. 'Do you want to get married, Helena? Will you marry me?'

5

Luanda: December 2006

PERHAPS IT WAS JUST THE ALCOHOL but Ana felt happy leaving Lena's house, so full of joy she wondered at her capacity for sadness, for desperation. Thinking maybe this was the compensation, that her life would always swing between extremes of emotion. She remembered how night would fall soon, and suddenly, as she walked along, gently humming a song. Wondering what Cristina was cooking for dinner and remembering the first time she'd gotten drunk during the day as a teenager, drifting into bed for a nap early that spring evening, then getting up and losing herself in John Huston's *The Dead*.

It's good to have some time off though, isn't it? she thought, sighing, remembering the hundred or so essays she'd had to get through before she could get away, and the extra pieces of work she'd taken on here and there; no weekends to speak of really since August. Oh, she wasn't complaining; she got paid to talk about film, to research it, open minds up to the medium, but so much of her time was given over to it. Bleary-eyed as she slipped between the sheets every night, mind turning, whirring, and always behind schedule, scrambling to finish books, articles, slides for her lectures.

When she got back to the apartment Tiago and Cristina were waiting for her. 'We're eating out tonight,' Cristina told her. 'A friend is going to look after the girls. We'll take you to a nice Chinese restaurant.' She grinned as she headed for her bedroom, leaving Ana slightly thrown off balance, wishing they'd told her earlier, that they hadn't just sprung this upon her.

This mausoleum of a place, with the air-conditioning turned up full and miles of tables covered in starched white cloths, only a few customers and the waiters overly attentive to their requests, facial expressions set in smiles of half-panic. But soon she began feeling much better about the evening out, left her anxiety behind, and though she hadn't planned on drinking any more, she soon got into the swing of things with this couple escaped from the confinement of their kids for a night. Until they all three had kicked back: laughing, joking, telling stories.

'That's Rodrigues,' Tiago pointed out a fat man in the corner. 'Has a big internet contract with the government.' Ana looked over at the middle-aged man and the under-the-table footsie he was playing with a girl much younger than herself.

'I wonder where his wife is tonight,' Cristina tutted. 'Look at him: fat, ugly, and he thinks he's King of the World because he has a bit of money and a young girl on his arm.' Tiago smirked and said nothing. 'And her, look at that dress,' she added, making Ana glance quickly at the full, dark breasts about to fall from the orange fabric, but not quickly enough to escape the dirty stare she was given in return.

And normally Ana would have looked away, but tonight,

feeling reckless, indifferent, she decided she wouldn't be intimidated by this badass act. Just leaned back in her chair and met the gaze head-on, thinking who was she anyway, using her ass…ets for all she could get. She looked and looked until she turned away, the other female, training her eyes back on her companion, leaving Ana a quiver of satisfaction.

After dinner was finished they decided they'd go on to a bar, join Helder, a friend of Tiago's. 'You wouldn't know the chaos of the city from here,' the former said to Ana an hour later, running his hand across the sky. 'You could be in New York, San Francisco.' She nodded, sitting by the water, taking in the lights glistening around the bay. Before she turned and saw her brother look two beauties up and down, their long legs, Beyoncé hair and dresses that had come from London, Paris, Brazil. She made herself focus on Helder again. 'I'm going to get a drink,' he was saying. 'Cutty Sark and Coca-Cola for you, no?' She nodded as he got up, leaving her listening to the music vibrating along the wooden floor, American R & B tunes. She began to tap her feet and move her body to the beat.

Thinking she was here, truly here in Luanda, as images from the past few days slowly began moving through her mind: all the buildings under construction, all the buildings falling down – Luanda. The men and women wedging themselves into the tiny, blue *candungero* buses – Luanda. Abandoned children with nowhere to go, walking along the city's streets – Luanda. The statue of Queen Jinga looking over the craziness of Kinaxixi Square – Luanda. And the broken windows of the apartments, bullet holes in the walls, beggars in wheelchairs, without legs, asking for money because it was Christmas – Luanda. The whole city seemed to be moving, faster and faster. All colour, noise and dust; three girls clicking their fingers, black Madonnas of the *musseque*.

Until Ana suddenly found herself standing by the water, leaning on the wooden railing and sobbing into the ocean. Confused, shoulders shaking, her back turned to the crowd. Before she felt Tiago's touch, heard him pleading, 'What happened? What's wrong, Ana?' And she tried to stop herself, warned herself not to go there, but it was no use, the words came tumbling out. 'I want to find her, Tiago. I want to find Solange.'

Oporto: December 1966

JOHNNY HALLYDAY ON THE TURNTABLE as José takes to the floor again. '*Retiens la nuit*,' he mouths the words to Helena as if she were Catherine Deneuve and he had a guitar in his hand, serenading her; '*Retiens la nuit pour nous deux jusqu'à la fin du monde.*' Moving slowly, snake-hipped, across the polished floor: jacket off, slightly drunk.

She's sitting with a friend from the student residence who casts her eye over the groom and thinks isn't Helena the lucky one, with this fine-looking man to lay her down tonight. Take the orange blossoms from her headdress and make love to her for hours. Helena watches José and grins broadly, tries not to explode into a fit of the giggles. Not because he is a bad dancer, moving out of time to the beat. No, it's just there is something of the fool, the court jester, about her new husband and his parody of a pop songster. But still, he looks now like he believes in the emotions behind the song, the romance of two young lovers.

Yes, he's happy, José: full of energy, of good will, centre-stage the way he likes it, as various sets of eyes watch him on the dance floor, causing him to perform, to play even more, lit up by the spotlights of their gaze. There's Auntie

Emília; fat fingers and fork poised over her third helping from the dessert table, face bright with pride at her little Zézinnho. And her sister Regina, mother of the groom, thinking, thank God her youngest has got sorted out with somebody and that you really couldn't ask for a nicer girl than Helena. While across the room is cousin Esmeralda, soft on him when they were kids, back on the beaches of their childhood. She's studying chemistry in London now and living with her boyfriend, but telling nobody except José. Old pal José, she giggles with the boldness of it, revealing the truth while they smoke a cigarette together.

And Helena's mother, Helena's mother is somewhere out there, smile-frowning. Old sour face; can't deny her son-in-law is well-mannered, charming and not bad to look at, but there is something that worries her about him. Something male and treacherous behind his smiles, something of her husband. And she can't quite get her head around how quickly all of this has happened; the courtship, engagement and marriage, the fact that in a few weeks Helena will be gone, gone to Angola.

Helena relaxes into her chair and sings back to José as his lips curl silently around a French word. She's thinking of Angola, Luanda; sun on her skin in January and a whole new adventure before them. There's her job in a primary school there, the apartment they will rent, and the two of them building a life together. A baby in the next few years, she hopes. And all of this: the wedding preparations, the long reception, standing inside the Capela das Almas this morning, then getting their photograph taken outside against the blue and white tiled façade, all this is really about their future, their possibilities. As he takes her hand to dance, she can feel her heart aching for him, breaking for him, as she steps into his sway.

Soft, fragrant, that's how she feels to his touch, as he rests his other hand on the lace of her grandmother's wedding dress. She seems so small, so precious, he never wants to hurt her. Hopes to go on loving her the way he does tonight, lilt of the music, the wine, the living. Not thinking anything, just going along with it, allowing himself to be carried away.

And later, as they lie naked together in the bed of the hotel room, after they've made love, she runs her hand through his hair. While he looks at her and smiles, wondering if he was good enough, or if he should have taken longer to linger over her body, exploring it for hours and taking her slowly, agonisingly, to oblivion, instead of getting carried away with his thrust, his lust.

He tells himself to stop worrying just because it wasn't as wild as those post-midnight teenage trysts with the young widow who lived two floors above his family. Or as able to shape shift time and space as those afternoons with Alicia in her little flat in Alfama, smoking a cigarette in bed as the daylight was drained from the white room, looking at the picture of Elizabeth Taylor taped to the wall, next to her own photographs of faces from the district.

Because there was something extraordinary about Helena's trusting, naked wetness and the touch of their bare bodies together, something so natural about ending up in this room with her. 'Je t'en supplie à l'infini, retiens la nuit.'

6

Luanda: December 2006

'I HAVE TO GO OUT AND DO A FEW THINGS. Want to come?' Cristina invited Ana the next morning. If the truth be known, she didn't, but the prospect of staying in the apartment seemed more oppressive, shutters closed against the blazing sun. 'The girls are going to stay with Bia,' Cristina put a finger to her lips and nodded in the direction of the bedroom where Ana could hear them talking to the woman who sometimes came to clean and take care of them.

'Okay,' she accepted, 'just give me a minute,' and went to the mirror to put on some red lipstick and brush her hair quickly.

They went to the bakery first, a drive-in where Cristina paid for three bags of bread rolls through the car window. Enough to get them through the Christmas break, or so she hoped. Ana remained indifferent; just stared out the window until they got to the supermarket, then trailed the other woman through the big warehouse of a place, gazing up at boxes stacked to the ceiling and walking into the cold storage room, plastic strips of curtains slapping back together behind her. She could have, should have, offered to cook dinner that night, gone and rounded up the ingredients for her dish, but couldn't really be bothered. Besides, it struck her that Cristina might not jump at the prospect, that she liked things done her way and if Ana *did* cook something her sister-in-law might spend the duration of the preparation peering over her shoulder, feigning interest but criticising, really, what she was doing.

No, she didn't have the resources now for that small battle of wills and trying to prove herself, her worth, through the food she put on the table. Later, in a few days, she'd make something magnificent, but right now her head was throbbing and there were people pushing past her. Taking a deep breath would have made sense, but all she could think of was tearing somebody to pieces, like an animal carcass, her own insides feeling as though they were pulling apart. She dug her nails into the flesh of her left arm and bit her lip, hoping Cristina wouldn't be too much longer, thinking of those evening hours in supermarkets with Helena when she was a girl. Until they finally got to the tills and the slim, beautiful, impossibly young girls working behind them.

As soon as they were in the car Ana opened a Coca-Cola and took a long gulp of it. Thinking how horrified some of her pseudo-hippie friends in Dublin would be to see her drinking the evil syrup. She was trembling slightly and made a rasping sound as she took the can down from her lips, evidence of the night before crawling through the moisture of her skin. 'Are you okay?' Cristina asked.

'Yes, fine,' she replied, noticing the slice of defence in her voice as soon as she said it, regretting it for a moment but thinking, of course I'm not okay, of course I'm not, as the puppets of despair danced in her stomach and she wished she'd never come to Angola.

Her sister-in-law said nothing, just moved the car back

out onto the road. 'I have to go to the Italian supermarket as well,' she said casually, 'won't take long.' 'Okay,' Ana tried to resign herself to the next mind-numbing task, looking out at the city; the hologram of Che Guevara on the back windscreen of a jeep in front, the bright red and yellow colours of a billboard villager encouraging the population to register for next year's elections. If they ever happened!

She caught a glimpse of Cristina and wondered if Tiago had asked her to keep an eye on her while he was at work, after the antics of the previous night, but the thought was interrupted. 'Is there anything you want?' Cristina asked as they arrived at their next destination, rabbiting on about all of the products they had.

'I'll take a look,' Ana made a weak attempt at diplomacy and wondered, as they went inside and Cristina began to stock up on pasta and tins of tomatoes, if this was her daily life. If her only outlet were these long aisles where Asian housewives and their Angolan drivers wandered, where English women with loud voices blended like rice pudding into the blandness of the place. And if this was how she lived then Ana couldn't understand how she didn't go out of her mind, suffering this *Jeanne Dielman* existence, going from cooking lunch to washing up, to preparing dinner and getting the kids ready for bed, then drifting there herself, exhausted. And why does she seem to thrive on it, to relish the prospect of another day to be organised A to Z? Ana asked herself.

Oh, she shouldn't have been judging, she knew that, but maybe that's exactly what her sister-in-law was doing herself, as she placidly paced the shelves, *haus frau* of the year. Thinking she knew from the moment Ana phoned Tiago to say she was coming that there would be trouble.

That his little sister would quickly take centre stage, silently calculating her way towards an explosion that would leave her husband devastated.

Maybe she's right, Ana sighed. Perhaps I do need to be the centre of attention. She imagined the shame pulsing through the veins of one arm as they left the place and remembered that it would be Christmas in a few days as she noticed the enormous bow done in green, white and red crepe paper at the front door. 'How strange to be in the sun at Christmas,' some other foreign body might have stated, unthinking, but there were stranger things in life, Ana knew, so she said nothing.

Just looked out from behind the glass and heard Cristina speaking again, 'I want to drop two presents into the girls' teachers,' as they drove away from the bay and up a hill. 'One of them said she'd be at the school anyway.'

'Okay,' Ana smiled, relaxing momentarily. 'Is it good, the school?'

'Yeah, most of the teachers are good. Though there are a few that shouldn't be there. No interest in the kids,' Cristina replied. 'It's gotten very popular, you know, in the last few years. We were lucky to get Belita in.'

'Is that right?' Ana asked.

'Yes, and the prices have gone way up. But the English language school across the road,' she whistled, 'you'd want a gold mine to pay…'

'What's that? Sorry,' Ana interrupted, as they moved along a white wall.

'It's a cemetery. Very old,' Cristina responded.

'Oh, can we go there on the way back? I'd like to see it,' Ana requested, so suddenly engaged with the prospect she hardly noticed Cristina's body freeze slightly away from her.

Or the 1920s straight angles and squat buildings of the school when they entered the grounds. Though there was the drift of a thought of Helena, the primary school teacher, as a kind of Deborah Kerr out here in tropical Africa. But that was all, just those clouds of thought passing before her eyes as she smiled and said hello to one of the teachers, to the secretary, to the woman who was cleaning the toilets where she went to pee.

'Do you want me to come with you?' Cristina proposed as she pulled up by the cemetery half an hour afterwards.

'No. I'll be fine, thanks,' Ana smiled. Then turned quickly and jumped out of the jeep, wondering at the sense in all of this, knowing she wasn't seriously going to trawl through all of these headstones to see if any were carved with the name Solange Mendes. But there she was, subject to the stares of the gravediggers who each stopped their work in turn to look after her wiry frame, walking along the lines of Portuguese names, pausing here and there to take one in: Mendes, João (1900–1982), Mendes, Isabel (1853–1921), Mendes, David (1954–1964).

This place must be for the rich bags of bones, Ana thought as she moved along, recalling photographs of civil war graves she'd seen and how different they were to these. Those mounds of earth, marked with handmade wooden crosses. She remembered then, as she trod the crooked pot-holed paths, another cemetery, that one in Oporto, and a spring morning when she was ten or eleven and they laid Helena's mother down in the earth. Holding her father's hand and watching the procession of people to the grave-side, the older women with fine black spiderwebs laid on their hair, shedding tears on beautiful handkerchiefs saved up for a death like this. Wondering herself if she should cry, at least make a show of crying, or whether to set her face grim and solid like the men who seemed oblivious to the drama unfolding all around them, even Senhor Fonseca just looking blankly down at the hole in the ground.

In fact, the only man with emotion on his face was her father and what Ana saw wasn't good, wasn't natural. They'd had an argument, this time with words, out loud, on the drive up, Helena suddenly losing all control, shouting at him, really roaring at him, then kicking the car and slamming the door when he stopped. 'You're not a man, you're not a decent man,' she'd said. Just after he'd proposed casually, offhand, that maybe they could stop somewhere to eat, saying he was exhausted.

Now she was standing slightly apart from her husband, Helena, the row turned to wordless recriminations and a clear warning signal that he should keep his distance. Silence again, but there was something about the way she stood by that grave, not looking at him, that smeared itself like a bloody injury across his face, made him seem so small, so useless, all Ana wanted was to kick her in the shins. But instead she stood, aware; oh yes, aware, of the odd over-curious glance aimed in her direction.

And later that day, back at the big, dark apartment where Helena had grown up she spent the afternoon in an agony of dreadful expectation. Waiting, waiting, for one of the adults – and it could be any one of these heeled women or besuited gents – to look down at her and ask what her name was, who she was. The terror of it left her paralytic in a corner for hours, her father unable to protect her now, off beside his own mother. Leaving Ana with her thoughts turning, tummy twisting as she imagined what she would say in reply should she be approached, trying to come up with something so that she wouldn't just curl up and die of shame like an old cat in the corner. But how could she respond to the question of how she was related to that stranger they'd sealed in a wooden box and put in the damp soil.

Because any time she'd met the shrinking old woman, she'd only betrayed her feelings with the occasional disdainful glance. No, Ana hadn't liked her, not really, not since the afternoon she'd looked at all the photographs on the walls of the woman's apartment and found her own face missing. Even if she had retained a soft spot for the husband, who was always doing the wrong thing, wearing the wrong tie. Who'd lived in Angola himself for a couple of years but had moved back to Oporto for the devastating charms of Fernanda Machado. Who was all dead now, not that Ana gave a damn.

Paris: December 1966

TAKE YOUR SEATS LADIES AND GENTLEMEN.
ALLEZ, ALLEZ!

Godard   Comedy   Legrand   Drama   de Castro   Paris
Eastmancolor   Coutard   Lubitsch   Guillemot   Allen
Cinéma

15th December 1966

Helena   **de Castro**   **José**

Honeymoon in Paris

Lights, camera, action!

… as José and Helena walk across the bridge to Notre
Dame Cathedral and the Île de la Cité. Stroll around the
church with the other tourists, and there are some, even
though it's freezing cold this Tuesday afternoon. Deep
winter grey but oh, it's still beautiful, Paris, with shop fronts
glowing blue, yellow and red against the day, just like the
tangerine of Helena's woollen winter coat.

They've spent two days walking the city already, will

continue wandering until it's time to go home: from the Quartier Latin to Saint-Germain, to Les Halles and Pigalle. All along the banks of the Seine, the mid-winter *mise-en-scène* of the city suddenly making sense as they pause on bridges and take in shots of rows of old buildings against the water. And what bridges; crossing back and forth and dreaming of the splendour of carriages passing this way in the years before the revolution.

Sometimes the photographs they take show the two of them in front of famous landmarks; the Louvre, the Eiffel Tower, Sacré Coeur, but other times there's just one of them, or neither, just the place. Or the subjects are anonymous: a bakery window, an old jukebox in a café, a poster for a jazz concert, the façade of an unnamed building, hundreds of years old.

But really it's the scenes from back in the hotel room that tell the story of that week. Where they go some late afternoons to make love, as darkness steals silently down into the city. Those silly snaps of José with hat tilted, sunglasses on and lips sullen like Belmondo playing Bogie. Or Helena with a beret, conjuring up Michèle Morgan in *Quai des brumes*. Both of them laughing at their foolishness, but glowing with this closeness, this warmth, this intimacy, discovering the city like two pals, two partners in crime.

They make love again that Thursday, José not bothering to close the curtains, thinking nobody will be able to see anything with just the dim glow of the lamp, and if they do, then let them. Let them see two lovers lying down. Sweet, slow and it's getting better, this act of love, felt divine there for a moment, police siren in the distance and time hanging in the air, unmoving.

Afterwards they fall asleep, then wake up, wash, dress,

and head out to a fancy restaurant, but decide to eat instead at a brasserie on the same street as the hotel. With an interior that is bright red velvet and dark stained wood. And after they've ordered, as they wait for their food, sip at the wine, José asks, 'Do you think we look like newlyweds?'

'I don't know,' Helena laughs, looking around then and out at the wet street outside. 'I suppose we might as well enjoy it. In a few weeks I'll only be good for making your dinner.'

'And getting my slippers, of course, when I come home from work,' he jokes.

'I wonder how we'll play it though,' she says after a pause.

'Play what?' he asks.

'Oh, you know, the marriage. I mean, should we go for a comedy or a tragedy?'

He watches a smile inch its way across her lips. 'You never know these days,' he shakes his head. 'But let's not think about that. It's time for a musical number.'

And with the click of his fingers Françoise Hardy's voice thrills into the room, *Il est tout pour moi*, as the couple move their shoulders to the beat. While all the other patrons watch and witness, a fleeting moment of love.

FIN

7

Luanda: December 2006

THEY HADN'T PLANNED on having a party that night, Christmas night, Tiago and Cristina, but that didn't matter, wasn't the way things worked anyway, out here in Angola. He just put it to his wife, as Ana lay on the couch with the girls watching *The Wizard of Oz*, tired from the meal and celebrations the night before, that maybe they could ask Carlos and Deolinda over for a drink later. Margarida and Zé as well, if they were around. 'Is that Carlos you went to school with?' Ana called over to her brother as Toto ran into Miss Gulch's garden.

'Yes, he came back just before I did. Has his own public relations company. Married Deolinda a few years ago. Have you ever met her?'

'No, I don't think so,' Ana replied.

'Keeps him under the thumb, you know,' Tiago whistled.

Ana smiled, thinking of Carlos and her brother, how wild they'd been when they were younger; drinking down on the beach, doing lines of cocaine off the kitchen table when their parents were out, with a string of girls chasing them, changing by the month. Carlos, whose father was still in Angola, his mother threatening to send him straight back there if he didn't start behaving, but knowing she wouldn't, that however bad he was in Portugal, he would be worse there. With that father who wouldn't do a thing to keep him under control, indifferent to everything except his drink and women.

Carlos, long, gangly legs open as he'd slouched in a chair on their balcony in Carcavelos that night, hair left to grow into an afro. 'What teachers you got?' he asked Ana about St Julian's, where she'd recently moved to the secondary school, leaving Helena behind still teaching at the primary. And laughed as she went through the names, telling her some of the tortures they'd inflicted on the teachers: hiding Mr Robinson's briefcase, putting a mouse in mad old Ms Cohen's bag, painting Mr Kelly's face on a hard-boiled egg. Laughing, laughing deeply, calling over to Tiago.

And sure enough, there he was, years on, Carlos. Same way of sitting in a chair, sipping a *caipirinha* in Tiago's apartment and asking Ana if it was cold in Dublin, if the girls there were as wild as he'd heard. 'Yeah, they're pretty tough,' she grinned. 'And big, big girls, you know.'

'Oh yeah? And what do people do for fun there? Doesn't it rain all the time?'

'Drink,' she laughed.

'Sounds like my kind of place then, sister,' his eyes lit up.

'No, the people do drink a hell of a lot but there are other things to do as well: theatre, lots of music, and the food's even got better.'

'All right, the potatoes. Don't they eat them like five times a day?' he asked.

'Just about,' Ana grinned, looking over at Nina, Carlos's aunt, as she reached to take a handful of nuts from a bowl on the table, then at Nádia, her twin sister, coming from the kitchen, thinking Nina's glasses were the only way of telling them apart.

'I couldn't believe it when I first arrived,' she continued, 'potatoes with burgers, potatoes with fish fingers, potatoes with beans, chip sandwiches!' She laughed at the memory of her early days there. 'They even make a drink from potatoes, *poitín* it's called. So strong. I'd say you'd like it, Carlos.'

'Ehhh,' he slapped his thigh.

'Have you been living there for long?' Nádia asked as she sat down on the couch, looking straight at Ana.

'Thirteen years now,' she answered, saying, but not feeling, the number.

'And are you married there?' Nádia asked.

'No,' she smiled to herself at the woman's directness.

'Maybe you're better off. I've just got rid of my husband,' she sighed.

'About time too,' her sister muttered.

'Years of coming back to me, asking me to take him back,' Nádia again. 'Well, the divorce is through now at last and I'm a free woman.'

'Thank God for that,' cheered Nina.

'*Ó* auntie, I might be able to push a couple of guys your way. Good guys, you know, that you could marry,' Carlos teased his mother's sister.

'No thanks, dear, I'm going to enjoy myself for a while,' Nádia smiled suddenly, big, bright, changing her whole face.

'And children, don't you want children?' she turned back to Ana with another question, as her twin squirmed slightly, silently, next to her.

Children, she thought she wanted them some day, some days, but not just yet. Of course there *were* long hours when she felt the yearning, like these afternoons with Carolina and Belita, but other times there was nothing, absolutely nothing, kids completely off the radar. Or bleak moments of fear, of terror, with the thought that she would be no good to her baby if she ever had one. Would harm it somehow; neglect it or abandon it, walk back into her own life, own ego. 'Maybe in the future I'll have children, yes,' she answered finally, noticing it was Nina who seemed to be scrutinising her now.

'Too right,' Nina gave her opinion, surprising Ana with her tone. 'You're still young. How old are you, dear?'

'Thirty-one,' Ana replied.

'Loads of time, honey,' she waved her hand as if telling her not to worry about anything for now. 'That's the problem here. Women think that they have to have babies when they're so young. Told that's all they're good for. Tsssk.' Nina was on a roll now. 'And then the husband goes off looking for a younger model, a girl without any kids to have his fun with. I've seen it happen again and again and for the life of me I still can't understand why they put up with it.'

Carlos chuckled to himself. 'Don't be sore, auntie.' He looked at Ana. 'She's still fuming because some bushman broke her heart years ago. Isn't that right, auntie?' Nina shook her head, like she'd heard this hundreds of times before. 'So she went and married a Belgian dude, right?' Carlos continued. 'But they aren't like the Angolans, are they, auntie, those Europeans? Oh no,' he gyrated his crotch and behind as he went out to the balcony for a cigarette, Nina bursting into a sudden fit of the giggles despite herself.

'Get out of here,' Ana called to him, laughing, before turning back to Nina.

'So you don't live here in Angola?' she asked.

'Tsk, tsk, tsk, Nina hasn't lived here in years,' Nádia answered. 'She left back in '75, for Lisbon.'

'And that's where you live now?' Ana wondered.

'No, no, no, in Brussels,' Nina replied, wagging her finger. 'I met my husband when I went there to study for a year.'

'And you, Nádia, you stayed here?' Ana addressed the other woman.

'Yes, I've been here all my life, lived through the whole war,' she nodded her head.

'And why, why did you decide to stay?' Ana wanted to know.

'Why? Why *should* I leave?' the rhetorical question shot through the air, Nadia's big brown eyes widening adamantly and cheeks glowing bright. 'This is my home.'

There was a pause. 'I could have gone,' she continued, hands gesturing in front of her. 'I had a job, had relations in Lisbon, was supposed to leave with Nina. But then I thought, Why? Why am I allowing myself to be driven out? People were doing anything then: trading diamonds, cars, crates of beer just for an airplane ticket. And I had one, we had one each, were all set to go. But one evening I was standing on our balcony, just a few days before we were set to leave, watching everybody, all the cars, hurrying in a panic through the streets, and I said to myself, standing there, this isn't worth it. This is my home, my land. Let them come and kill me if they want. Let them tear down this house but I won't go.'

Ana thought for a moment of *Rome, Open City*: Anna Magnani breaking into the bakery, later telling Don Pietro she'd love to beat the German soldiers' faces in. She could feel her own imagination warming up. 'Was it really bad here at the time?' she put the question to Nádia.

'Eeeeeee, you can't imagine it!' the woman shook her head. 'It got very bad. Whole city full of rubbish because there was nobody to collect it, and there were dogs running wild on the streets. Their owners had gone to Portugal and left them. Then down by the port there were crates and crates of belongings to go onto the ships. With all of us waiting, waiting, waiting for something to happen. We didn't know what the Portuguese were going to do, if they'd really let go of Angola, and we were sure the FNLA were going to attack. Expecting, really expecting the end.'

Ana could feel her heart beating with excitement now. Inappropriate, she knew, but there it was, as she imagined José and Helena packing up his typewriter, her heart, their dream, knowing nothing could be the same again. Glimpses of the leaving they'd never spoken to the children about, their departure from that place they would shroud in silence but which was always somehow there. In José's lingering looks down towards the sea, in the pregnant blossoms out on Helena's balcony garden and in Tiago's nights out on the town, off his head. Gone, somewhere, over the rainbow.

'But at least there was a sense of community then, wasn't there?' Nina prompted her sister.

'Yes, yes,' Nádia replied, gazing at Ana. 'And Neto, Agostinho Neto was a real leader; the people were really behind him. He was a doctor, a poet, you know. We thought we had a real future with him.' She paused, then began speaking again. 'And we all had to get involved under the new government, it's true. There were teachers cleaning the streets, big businessmen sent to work on the coffee plantations. And we helped each other all the time, all through the war, the women. If somebody had some flour one week, she'd share it with the rest of us. The same if somebody else had some meat or chicken. We shared everything.'

She chuckled loudly, 'I remember one time a whole ship full of hens arrived out of nowhere in Luanda.' She took a breath. 'Well, for the whole month everybody lived on eggs: fried, boiled, scrambled, poached, you name it. The city smelled of eggs for weeks. Whole city smelled of eggs.'

The three women laughed, as Carlos handed them all another drink, before sitting down with his guitar, strumming, singing softly.

An hour before Ana took the room with her own particular party piece. Opened her mouth to sing, '*Eu não sou daqui*'. The way she did in Dublin now and then, at parties when some smiling, sad-eyed Irishman would ask her to sing something in Portuguese.

It was only in Dublin she had begun to sing out loud. That night after a *sean-nós* singer, sitting hands on knees in a smoky corner of The Cobblestone, had split her heart and made her happy somewhere behind the tears she refused to cry. Thinking of a tune for the sing-song that was sure to start up back in the house as she and her friends emerged into the sodden streets, rainwater trickling diagonally down the old walls of the fallen-down pub.

And now here she was, years later, the whole room singing along with her, all the candles in the apartment flickering against the deep, dark sky of Luanda. '*Marinheiro só*.'

Luanda: January 1967

SILENCE, ALL THE LIGHTS TURNED DOWN, as José and Helena step onto the beach and into the widescreen Technicolor of the frame. Of the Ilha de Luanda, where they've come to spend a day at the sea. Having driven around the sweep of the bay, roof down: past the boat club, the zoo.

When their feet hit the sand their shoes come off, as they try to find a spot among Sunday couples and scores of families; all lying, sitting, swimming, eating, talking, taking in the sun. And as he puts on his blue trunks he feels a stirring in his groin, same feeling every year first trip to the beach: the sudden swarm of near-naked bodies, the repetitive hush of the sea and the knowledge of his own flesh. His heart still beats fast at the surprise of it all, though he should be used to it by now; all those summer Sundays spent on the string of beaches towards Cascais and out at Caparica. But still it gets him every year.

Helena lays out the navy blanket on some empty sand she finds, not too close to anyone else, watches José looking out at the world, child in a sweet shop, as if he's never seen the sea before. She feels a hazy desire for him stretch along the inside of her leg and into her stomach, notices how pale he looks against the dark brown flesh all around. '*Olha branco*, would you like something to eat now?' she asks him.

'No, I think I'll go for a swim first,' he answers. 'Do you want to come?'

'Do you think we can leave the things here?' she wonders. 'Will they be okay?'

'Yeah, fine. I'll ask them to keep an eye out.'

And he walks over to a couple in their fifties, asks them politely to watch their belongings while they go for a swim. 'Of course, son,' the woman says from beneath her canvas sun hat, sandwich in hand. 'The water's nice today,' the man recommends, 'I was in myself earlier.'

'Fantastic,' José says, thanks them and strolls slowly back to Helena. Who is taking her sunglasses off and sliding the pink hairband from her hair.

And as she pulls the yellow cotton dress over her head José notices a couple of men taking the scene in, and how unaware Helena seems of their naked looks. Making him feel suddenly proud, then protective, then somehow jealous of their lascivious glances. Before he becomes aware of the movement of his own sex and forgets what he was thinking.

But she knows they're eating her up all right, these men whose eyes wander the length of the beach. And it's not that she feels either flattered or incensed; they're just men after all, men taking their visual fill; she's used to it by now, thinks very little about it. She's no *Gilda*, that's true, all set to put on a show for them, but neither is she a prude, buttoned up to prying eyes. No, what she's more concerned about now is the pallor of her own skin. Oh, she might have teased José but if the truth be told she feels like a piece of goat's cheese here on the beach, freckles ready to breed by the hour. Wishing, at times like these, she was like everybody else, with their lively suntans and healthy hues. Instead of having to slather on sun cream before she's even left the house, banished from the sun beneath the shadow of a big red and white striped umbrella.

'Are you ready, my dear?' his shadow passes in front of her.

'Yes,' she snaps out of her useless reverie, puts out her hand. And as she moves, she falls into his arms and kisses him for a moment, uncaring suddenly if anybody has any comment to make. Thinking they have left all of that behind: the gossiping neighbours, the bitter relations, that whole damp, dreary place, Lisbon. They're in the modern world, a much more modern city now, and if anybody cares to stare, then let them.

And, as if catching the sudden recklessness racing through her, he runs his hand over her bottom, covered by the cloth of a nautical swimsuit. Before he takes her hand again and they stroll down to the water. Pausing at its edge as if expecting the shock of the Atlantic during a spring afternoon in Portugal. But no, it's warm, so nice and warm, as she, then he, wade in.

8

Luanda: December 2006

SO, THIS IS IT, ANA THOUGHT as Tiago's jeep jerked up again, down again, the point where the European city ends and the African one begins. Or once did. Red earth and unpaved roads, dust clouds brought to life by his tyres, she could only imagine what it looked like when it rained.

She tried to fit the place into her mind's map of Luanda, looking at houses with forest-green walls and red window frames, others painted contrasting shades of blue, then uglier cement shacks. Though all she was feeling really that she was tired of this charade, wishing she'd never called Luísa, Lena's friend, never charmed her into meeting her to talk about this mother, this other life she wasn't sure she was all that interested in today.

A nothingness, a stubborn, worn-out nothingness, that was all she felt now. Lena, Nádia and Nina, all of the others, the search had come to nothing thus far. So why was she here again, with her photocopy, that battered stolen second of time? Like some circus freak traipsing from town to town with this touchstone, this talisman.

And sucking the life out of Tiago again, who'd promised to help her, said he'd do anything he could to help her find

Solange, after that night she'd broken down like a Douglas Sirk heroine in the bar. He was sitting now in a respectful veil of silence beside her, but all she could think was that she'd trapped him once more in the meaningless web of her moods. Why do you have to be so difficult, so hostile? she wondered, and crawled around her head for anything she might ask him, tell him. 'Do you want to come with me?' the words came from nowhere, surprised Ana herself.

Tiago looked even more puzzled; then considered, really thought about it for a moment, looked like he was about to say something before he veered away from it. 'No, I'm okay. I have a few things to do. I'll pick you up afterwards. Just call me. We can have a beer.'

'Okay,' Ana leaned over to kiss him goodbye, wishing she could go off with him, wherever he was going, or lose herself alone in the city; but she steeled her will against the urge, straightened her back and moved the red frames of her sunglasses down onto her nose, fingers brushing against silver hoop earrings. She slammed the door of the jeep and stood outside the small house where they had stopped, walls the blue and grey stained pink of a January twilight in Dublin.

And it was she who made the first move when a woman opened its front door, then unlocked the metal gate in front of it. Brushing the soft skin of both cheeks with her lips before introducing herself, 'I'm Ana.' She stood back and took Luísa in: tiny frame, hair caught back with conditioner combed through it, sad or happy brown eyes, she couldn't tell; but sensitive anyway. Suddenly she felt somehow maternal, heart straining at the sight of this woman, who responded, smiling, 'I'm Luísa. Come on in.'

'You're from Portugal, aren't you?' she asked as Ana moved inside.

'Yes, that's right, from Lisbon,' she confirmed.

'Ah, my father was from Portugal too, from Coimbra. A Republican, sent here to Angola as a political exile.' There was a look of pride, of cheer on her face.

'Coimbra's very beautiful, isn't it?' Ana commented. 'You've been there, haven't you, Luísa?'

'*Sim,* senhora,' the woman asserted, 'I sang a lot in Portugal, spent six months in Lisbon. *Eh pá!* A lifetime ago.'

'And do you still live in Lisbon, Ana? Sit down, sit down please,' Luísa soothed. 'Let me get you a drink.'

'No, in Ireland, Dublin. And I'll just have a coffee if that's okay.'

'*Claro*, of course it's okay,' Luísa called over her shoulder as she shuffled off to the kitchen, the soles of her flat, brown leather sandals slip-slapping against the cracked tiles of the floor. 'I've never been to Ireland. London *sim*, but Dublin no.' Ana smiled at how she pronounced the cities' names. 'Are there many Angolans there?' she called from the kitchen.

'Some,' she answered, thinking of the bright green barbershop near her house and her sidelong gazes inside it; at men hunched over with laughter, sitting there for hours, with women running their fingers through long extensions, and the little girl in fake heels and plastic jewellery walking round and round. In rain, snow or on long June evenings it was the musk and heat and sound of Angola she always imagined inside that shop, never once going in.

She slid along the couch and over to the fan, pushing the mass of curls off her shoulders, sweltering already, quickly looking under the armpits of her peasant blouse for sweat patches. Thinking of celebrities she'd seen named and shamed in trashy magazines, condemned for perspiring in public. She felt relieved that she wouldn't be found guilty just yet and decided to go to the kitchen to ask Luísa for a glass of water as well. She lifted herself from the sofa, taking in all the plants around the room as she went towards the kitchen; the palms, the orchids, the cacti erotically unfurled over coloured clay pots. And almost walked smack-bang into the tiny woman, rolling back from the kitchen like a freight train now, a piece of yellow material spattered in flowers pink, green and blue in her hands.

'You have a bit of Angola in you too, no?' she looked at Ana for a moment. Just like the tablecloths in that café in Rio de Janeiro, Ana remembered, as Luísa placed the fabric over the wooden coffee table, nimble fingers smoothing it out and tugging at its edges.

'Yes, yes,' she confirmed. 'My mother was Angolan.'

The other woman put a hand on her hip. 'That's right. Lena told me.' There was a long, hollow silence and Ana wondered which one of them should speak. 'Hold on a moment. I won't be a minute. Just let me finish this,' Luísa was off to the kitchen again. 'You want some water as well, right?'

'Yes, that would be good,' Ana called back.

'Now,' she sighed a few minutes later, the table set with an old silver coffee pot, delicate-looking cups and saucers, 'tell me.' More striking really next to the tacky red and green sugar bowl, the milk jug with a chip in it. Luísa continued stirring her coffee, then rested it on the arm of the big chair she leaned back into, which was covered in a large piece of fabric, blue seashells against a brown shore, and continued speaking. 'You're here looking for your mother. Lena thought I might be able to help. Ask me what you want, darling.' Ana noticed then how deep her voice was, thought how she'd love to just sit here and talk to this woman, sing with her perhaps. Before she told herself to get a grip.

'Yes, it's my mother,' she confirmed, the M word running through her head: My mother, *A minha mãe, Mi mamá, Ma mère*. 'I've never met her. Well, not since I was very, very young,' she looked directly at Luísa, 'but my brother is living in Luanda now and I thought since I was coming to see him I might try to find her.' She wondered, as she spoke, why she'd said it like that, thought that wasn't really true, or was it, and chided herself for being so falsely casual. Pressed herself again as to when it was she'd definitively decided to look for her, if it was the holiday or the search that had really come first.

'And her name was Solange, was it?' Luísa looked at her, encouraging her to go on. Snapped Ana out of whatever swift, stupid battle she was about to get into with herself, chasing the truth of decisions and choices that didn't really matter. Enough, a silent voice in her head and then words again, real words; calm, confident, so casual.

'Yes,' she noticed how petite Luísa was again, slim legs poking out from her green and yellow dress, 'that's right. I suppose she was very young when my father met her. He was married to another woman, you see. Portuguese as well. They moved here together in the sixties.'

Luísa shook her head. 'It happened a lot here, happened a lot,' she gave Ana a smile of empathy. 'The women, the African women, they're different from the Portuguese, you know,' she smiled. 'White men always came to the *musseques*, went with prostitutes or just normal women. And some of them really took advantage, you know, got the girls pregnant, then just walked away, back to the paved city, leaving those *mulatas* to grow up without fathers. And then what was left for these girls to do except sell themselves when they were older? It's a shame, I tell you, a shame. Tut, tut, tut. Thanks be to God my father wasn't like that. He loved this country, not like some of the whites. But tell me about Solange.'

'All I know is that my father had a relationship with this girl,' Ana managed to reply, though what she was really thinking about was that word, that possibility, prostitute. Dirty, dark, wild. 'He got her pregnant and they took me with them when they left, a year or so after independence, when they went back to Portugal,' she felt sick again with the invisible thoughts trickling through behind her words, that school-day shame that her mother might be like one of those women who sold themselves against dilapidated buildings near Cais do Sodré station. That this was all she'd come from, added up to.

'So you haven't seen your mother in all this time?'

Ana shook her head. 'No. All I really know is that she's a singer, or used to sing back then, when my dad knew her.' There was the dreadful roar of a scooter zipping past outside as Ana leaned down to pick up her bag, took the photocopy from between the pages of her notebook and passed it over to Luísa.

She saw Luísa open the glasses hanging round her neck and put them on her nose, 'I think so, yes. I'm sure I know their faces.'

Her words startled Ana, pulled the colour from her cheeks. '*Sim*?' she searched for confirmation, doubting the woman, thinking she was probably too old to be so certain this soon.

Luísa took another careful look. '*Sim*, yes. They were cousins, used to sing with Zicko Povão over in Sambizanga. I didn't know them well, you know, they were much younger than me but I knew them to see. Beautiful…'

Luísa was interrupted as the front door opened and in walked a man dressed in a purple polo shirt and jeans, calling to a girl and boy who came running in after him. 'Good afternoon,' he nodded to Ana and smiled, checking her out quickly.

'Good afternoon,' she replied non-commitally, as he bent down to kiss Luísa. Great fucking time to arrive, she thought.

'Oh Nana, Nana, can we have a Coca-Cola?' the kids pleaded, pulling at Luísa's dress, and before Ana knew it she was gone into the kitchen again.

But later, not much more than a few minutes later, she had returned, was banishing the kids, 'Go, go out and play, but be careful, eh! Stay away from that Roberto down the street. He'll try and take your trainers again. Out, out,' she clicked her fingers, moving the boy who stood staring at Ana.

'*Tchau*,' Ana called after them, then took the glass of juice Luisa handed her.

'*Olha*, yes. I don't know anything about them, Ana, but I'm sure that was them,' Luísa sat down again.

'And this Zicko Povão, do you think he might know something?' Ana had already decided her next move. 'Is there any way I could go and see him, talk to him?'

Luísa looked at her a long moment, then clicked her tongue three times. 'He's dead, Ana. Killed by the government on the twenty-seventh of May,' she lowered her voice. 'Back in '77.' She formed a gun from her fingers, a gesture almost obscene in her hands.

'Killed?' Ana pressed, though she wasn't really asking about Zicko Povão, was more wondering about Solange and if they had taken her out too. 'And these women, these girls?'

'I don't know, don't know anything about these girls, dear,' Luísa shook her head. 'All I can say is that the government say some of these musicians were involved in the coup against them, in the factionalism. Some of them said things, sang songs the government didn't like, and Zicko was one of them. It's a shame. Zicko had such a beautiful voice. And Pedro, Pedro sang well too. It's a shame, daughter. A great shame,' Luísa shook her head once more and looked at the floor.

'But killed?' Ana was suddenly adamant.

'Yes, yes, it was ruthless. Really brutal. Old comrades killing comrades. Terrible, terrible. *Olha*, I can't say who was involved in the coup and who wasn't. But lots of people in the MPLA were killed; it was a real purge, a civil war within a civil war. And these guys too, like Zicko, who'd always supported the party in their struggle. You know Zicko had travelled around the country with the government just after independence. Crazy, no?' Luísa sighed.

'But do you know, do you know anything else? Surely you must know something about these girls,' Ana pleaded.

'*Olha*, Ana, I'm almost seventy now. I was around much earlier than Zicko and all these guys. I started out when the guerrillas were with the music, when we were all fighting and singing against the Portuguese. I don't know what happened later. Maybe they're not dead, maybe nothing happened to these girls. All I know is that it was a terrible moment, a bad, bad moment in our history.' Ana realised this was going nowhere, asked Luísa if she minded her smoking. 'No, no senhora. As you please,' she went to get Ana an ashtray.

'Listen, I have a couple of friends who knew Zicko and the others, maybe you can talk to them, they might know something,' she lifted her shoulders, gave Ana a helpless look when she returned. 'But now I have to put the dinner on. You like fish, right?' Ana wondered how to tell the woman that she would be going soon, had to leave, but the feeling slowly seeped through her that she didn't have to be anywhere at all really. 'You are going to have dinner with us, no, Ana?' she put her hand on her hip again and implored.

'Yes, yes of course. Let me come and help you.'

'No, no, no, no, no!' Luisa commanded. 'Sit here, take it easy. I can do it,' and she was off again to the kitchen, leaving Ana sitting on the couch, watching the traces of smoke disappear.

Luanda: March 1967

A SWELTERING NIGHT IN LUANDA. Dinner and drinks at a terrace when José's friend Eduardo suggests, 'Let's go to a club. Come on, let's have a dance.' Helena and Fátima are melting already but they both think why not, both like a jive. So they look at each other and agree. 'I'll take you to Maxinde,' Eduardo tells them. 'It's in the *musseque*. The *musseque* clubs are the only places to go if you want to have a dance, a real dance. Forget about the Portuguese city,' he makes a dismissive gesture with his hand as Helena sips the last of her gin and tonic.

And twenty minutes later in they walk, couples already filling the floor, mostly black but also a few white reflected in mirrors around the room. All the women are in new outfits, made especially for the night, the young men in tailored shirts, gyrating their bodies to the soothing beat of the band on stage, lead singer in a pristine suit, running his hand over his chest, the others behind him on trumpets, drums, guitars.

'What do you want to drink?' Eduardo asks, before José goes to help him with the two Cucas, the Coca-Colas for the ladies. Moves behind Eduardo, through the crowd, smiling at strangers, eyes suddenly opened wide to this other world; sweating, heaving, hip-shaking to life on Friday and Saturday nights. So different from where they live. There's a skinny girl in a short white dress dancing, ribbons in her hair, head hardly moving, shoulders, hips doing all the work, and José is fascinated by her. Thinks her extraordinary, then becomes conscious his eyes are prying and looks away. But back again as he rests an elbow on the bar, body coming slowly to life now with the music.

While Helena has placed her fingers lightly on Fátima's waist and is moving her body, manoeuvring it like the men do their girlfriends', wives'. It seemed so natural to take the woman's hand, to say 'Come on, let's dance,' with the whole place moving to the beat. Her partner is giggling too now, and as men rotate their chests and quietly cheer them on, Helena looks down at her smart shoes which are covered in dust, noticing the sweat trickling down her lower back. Feeling, so sure at this moment, that this is what they've come to Angola for.

José and Eduardo are coming back from the bar now, having been distracted by a friend of Eduardo's, an older gent. And as they near the two women Eduardo turns around to José. 'Look, look at this,' he says, indicating the sleek red shape of Helena's skirt against the black silk of Fátima's dress. 'Look, look, look,' he encourages as they rotate the hands held together, moving out from, then back into, one another. The song comes to an end then, singer taking a short sip of a drink and asking the audience if they're ready to dance now, to *really* dance now. '*Sim,*' they chorus back, a bare-chested man in Buddy Holly glasses already improvising without a beat.

The guitarist strums slowly, singer intones deeply and

the other men in the group respond, a slow lament of a song surely meant not for dancing. Until suddenly it explodes: the drums, the backing singers in *panos* winding their behinds, stage vibrating, club thumping. Jacket off, legs out and shoulders back, José bounces off the beat, shuffles over to Helena. Who puts a hand on her belly, holds another arm out at an angle, a one-two-three flash of feet into him, then out again, steps repeated twice before she chooses a spot and stands there, centred, moving only slightly, slowly now. While he cruises into the heavy thundering music, shoulders this way then that, feet tracing a swift pattern on the floor. And he's sweating hard and staring right at her as she makes him work. Surprised, surprised that she can dance to the tune so effortlessly, keep the beat, thought he'd be the one to lead her and here she is seducing him with her hips, barely making any effort at all.

9

Luanda: December 2006

ANA WONDERED WHAT IT MUST HAVE looked like, the downtown of this city, before independence, before the war, as they passed pavements where most of the cobblestones had been uprooted. Thought it must have been almost a real city back then, as she looked again at the destitute buildings, made out more random patterns of bullet wounds. Down one hill and along a main street where crowds of women in luminous fabrics waited for buses that might never come. 'Where did they live?' she asked without thinking. 'When they first came here?'

'Who?' Tiago answered from behind the wheel.

'I think she means your parents,' Cristina elaborated.

'Oh, not far from here,' he replied. 'I'll show you now.' He turned into one side street and then another.

Stopped a few moments later before an art deco building; once white, now grey, all its windows wide open or smashed, a pile of rubbish beside the entrance. 'I think this is it; I think this is the one Dad mentioned.' Ana looked out without emotion, wondering at what exact point in time the city had begun to die. Thinking about the fallibility of man, the vulnerabilities of his Babels, all of those vanished towns in the United States, once so full of hope, of life. Who says it can't happen, who says it can't? she asked herself. That any city, country can't be brought to the edge of extinction one day?

A flicker of an image of Lisbon: old mermaid, fin covered in barnacles and broken seashells, the façades of those buildings on the way to Santa Apolónia railway station. And the memory, again the impossible memory of this city, Luanda, as a place that was alive. With proper streets, cars, shops, cinemas. And José and Helena coming home from the beach late one Sunday afternoon, drawing the curtains. Where did it all go wrong? she thought to herself, watching them fleeing.

Before she caught sight of another beggar in a wheelchair, a 'Happy Holidays' cardboard sign around his neck, and told herself they were fools, fools. Just another couple of adventurers, tiny against the vastness of this place. 'Nothing good has ever come of Angola. Nothing good,' Ana could still taste the bitterness of Helena's mother's words overheard, as they passed by a magnificent old stone church, spun around the bay and to the boat yard where Tiago's friend would pick them up and take them to Mussulo.

Twenty minutes later she was putting a life jacket over her shoulders and tightening it at the waist, after she'd helped the girls on with theirs. She sat back in the boat, one long arm each for her nieces, Belita snuggling into her, before she moved them again to fix the knot of her headscarf, push the over-sized 1970s sunglasses up her nose and wipe an insect from her white linen trousers. 'White?' Cristina had looked at her from beneath an arched eyebrow earlier that morning. 'In Luanda?'

'But we're going to Mussulo, aren't we? It can't be as

dirty as the city,' Ana had answered, watching Cristina shrug her shoulders and continue packing the kids' clothes. Kids including Tiago, who seemed to be hypnotised by the rolling news on the TV.

Maybe she's right, Ana had thought, feeling a swift squirm of shame before she put it away, told herself not to doubt, to lose faith like this. That she'd spent long enough deciding what she was going to wear: the soft white flares, bright yellow silk shirt, the orange and brown headscarf she'd bought in a tiny shop off the Plaza Mayor in Madrid. And the glasses... 'You look like Senhora Bento,' Tiago laughed when she walked into the sitting room with her leather bag on her shoulder. 'Where did you get them, 1974?' Making Ana laugh too, unexpectedly, thinking what a bastard he was, her brother, but giving as good as she got. 'Same place as you got your haircut,' she answered. 'Now come on. Are we ready to go?'

And here they were hours later, sitting in Rui's boat. Rui, a decade older than Tiago but still handsome, not a bad body. 'Hold on,' he called out from behind the wheel, grinning like a boy. Ana squeezed the girls closer to her, '*Vamos.*' And as they drew slowly away from the city and out into the bay she felt her heart beat with excitement at the thought of this trip, a night at Rui's house in Mussulo.

She looked behind her, began thinking you wouldn't know, seeing the city from here, from this perspective, the madness of it, the chaos, the *confusão*.

Before she turned back around, tuning into the chugging of the boat, and thought of the projected backdrop behind Tippi Hedren as she takes the lovebirds across the bay; fur coat, green suit and perfectly styled blonde hair, legs to one side, ladylike. Tricksy Tippi.

Must be almost twenty years since Ana asked her father if she could stay up that night between Christmas and New Year, to watch this film she'd read about in the newspaper, *The Birds*. And only a couple of years since she watched it again for a lecture and really noticed all the content about mothers who are too close to their sons, and what Tippi says about her own missing mother.

She thought of the scene in the restaurant when the locals turn on Melanie and imagined Cristina whispering frantically to Tiago that night after she'd fallen apart at the bar, 'Why has she come? Why has she come?' as if she was the harbinger of death and destruction. There was a pang of regret before she asked Tiago what it was, that big white building that seemed to appear from nowhere, perched by the water on the Ilha, looking like the last word in 1960s sophistication.

'It's a hotel,' he roared above the engine, now running at full throttle.

'P A N O R A M A,' she read the big letters on its roof and reached for her camera. Zoom in, click, click, click, back out, click, click, then in again as Tiago went on. 'They say it used to be really nice, very elegant, back when it opened. But it's in bad shape now.'

'Oh yeah?' Ana prompted, still snapping away, a vague thought itching at the back of her mind.

'Yeah, I knew this Portuguese guy who was living here with his wife, but used to take another girl to the hotel for a bit of you know what,' he jigged his behind as Ana put the camera down. 'One evening he was there asleep and the girl started screaming, slapped him awake, telling him there was a rat in the corner,' Tiago's voice grew even louder as he got into the rhythm of the story, Cristina laughing already.

'Anyway, he got up and turned on the light. And there, in the corner, were two rats. This size,' Tiago demonstrated with open palms.

'Uggh,' Ana said, thinking of the rat she'd seen scurrying down the steps of a house on Parnell Square during the summer. 'Ugggggh,' Carolina and Belita repeated at almost exactly the same time.

'So he went down to reception to complain, this guy,' Tiago continued. 'Said there were two rats having a picnic in his room, that he wasn't paying two hundred dollars a night to share it with this vermin. He was really angry, you know, but the receptionist just looked at him, just sat there watching him, staring at him, until finally he asked, "How big were the rats, senhor?" "How big were they? Like this," the man said,' and Tiago opened his palms again. '"This big?"' Tiago imitated the receptionist copying the Portuguese man. '"Yeah," he said, "that big." "*Então*, you don't have to worry then," he told him. "If they were this size then you'd have something to worry about,"' the space between Tiago's hands widened to the length of a newborn baby, before he slapped his leg, laughing and shaking his head at the same time. 'Can you believe it?'

Ana could, just about, even if she'd only been in Angola a week. Though what interested her, really caught her imagination about the story, wasn't the punchline but the image of that girl sitting up in bed while her lover went to complain. Left alone as the middle-aged man, all paunch and half-hard prick, stuffed himself back into his underwear, ready to pounce with indignation, storming down to reception.

She looked out at the sea again, the open water they were zipping through, and imagined her ex-boyfriend Conor, wondered what he would say about the scene. Hoped he was okay, thought she must really call him when she got back to Dublin, but just as suddenly was brought back to the slimline girl on the bed, naked, knees up to her big breasts. Who is she? Where has she come from? she wondered, asking herself if she really was as frightened as she seemed or if this was all part of her performance, her spectacle of femininity; this calculated, continuing role as the delicate, beautiful lover. Because surely this wasn't the first time she'd seen a rat in Luanda. She knows what she's doing, must know. Just tits and ass and all that jazz, Ana thought silently as Rui slowed the boat down, told them they had to be careful here because there were sandbanks.

'They could ruin the bottom of the boat,' he said, hands still on the wheel as they glided along. He looked at Ana for a moment like he was thinking about something, considering something, then away. But what if that isn't the whole story? she reclined back into the infested lovers' suite. What if she does really like him? The girl again. Maybe she really thinks they have something? Just like Shirley MacLaine in *The Apartment*, waiting for Fred MacMurray to leave his wife.

But no, no woman with a body like that, lips like those, wouldn't know how to use them, she reasoned. What this girl really enjoys is the draw her legs have on his eyes, the effect of her behind on his dick; lick, lick, lick like his wife won't do. Just fun really, that's all it is, fun without consequences: these drives out to beaches when the tide is out, nights in rented rooms and the odd trip to Mussulo. Just an adventure for a girl from the *musseque*, flights away from her life and the city, and he looking like a fool t hinking he's holding the world in his dick in his hand. No consequences, and there are years left in this lean body yet if she continues to keep him keen enough to want to lose himself in her first thing on a Friday afternoon. Just two bodies; older, younger, making love around the Bay of Luanda.

Luanda: June 1967

THERE ARE DAYS, MANY DAYS like these, of course there are. When Helena leaves to cycle to school at seven in the morning, coming home in the afternoon and falling asleep with a book in her hand, before she wakes and begins dinner. Life is lived, and those first glimpses of the city fade as she is absorbed into it. Details, yes, details emerge; like the way people say *garina* instead of girl or the sharpness of the teeth of the Red Snapper, but there's mostly a falling away of those early thoughts and impressions; when the city, the country, could be seen as a whole. When family at home asked her what she thought of the place over the phone and she knew exactly what she wanted to say. She has a better sense of the place now, six months into their new life already, and yet she is less certain than before, isn't sure exactly how to describe it.

While for José a world, a way of life, has emerged, slipping into a new rhythm with those after-work drinks, conversations, Thursday and Friday evenings. Shaking the old order from his shoulders like sand from a towel in this corner of Africa, of Angola, where he is weightless next to the endless space that is opening up before him, so small against the heat, the history. And what gets him, really excites him, leaves him returning to a line in a clandestine novel again and again, is the Portuguese they use here, these Africans; the way they turn it inside out, stretch and twist the words, shoot it up with hot, sweet sun. Not like at home where everybody guards their words carefully, mean-spirited even with their tongues, reserving their flourishes for their whines and gripes. Sometimes it seems as though he's been reborn, reborn into a new language.

And Helena, what she likes is the ordinariness of her everyday life here, having a routine, a place she is useful, even if she is hesitant about socialising with the other teachers, as if she doesn't want anybody to have too much of a hold over her, doesn't want to belong to anybody. Not that they are unpleasant, her colleagues. They're nice, most of them anyway, even if there is so much spite Helena can detect going on beneath the questions muttered, the glances passed across the staffroom table; long, wordless moments left hanging for everybody to hear.

But it's not that she doesn't get on with them; more they don't interest her that much, not really. She just walks off into the afternoon every day telling whoever is left to have a good evening; rarely, very rarely, taking thoughts of any of them further than the threshold that cuts the school off from the outside world.

Thinking today how strange it is to have winter in June but that this isn't really a winter anyway, this dry season, this *cacimbo*. Even though some mornings the whole city seems shrouded in a white mist. But it's still not like the fog and slippery pavements of the city streets back home, deserted in December darkness.

It's Africa, Angola, Luanda they're putting into the

Portuguese, thinks José, these young writers, moulding, manipulating the mother tongue to their own devices. Colonising, civilising, the shiver of a thrill of a Luandino sentence, Kimbundu words, phrases skittering across history and time, taking their place on the pages of a book in another language. Sometimes he remembers, and sometimes he forgets, those writers who have been sent off to the prison camp of Tarrafal in Cape Verde, because of their political affiliations.

And sometimes, like today, Helena goes to places like Bairro Operário, cycles there after work. Then walks with her bicycle through the red earth of the streets, past tin houses painted blue with pillar-box red doors and windows, smiling brightly at old women. Letting the small girls that crowd around her touch her hair, run their fingers along the freckles and white skin of her arm, as their mothers look on and wonder if she is a force of good or evil.

And after she's left the area she might go home taking a new route, past the wall of the old cemetery, down the hill. Still wondering why their streets and houses were left like this and why it is she isn't teaching these children who really need her help, who don't seem to get much of an education. She thinks of Audrey Hepburn and her disappointment in *The Nun's Story* when she is told she will be working in the white hospital. She passes a military jeep, sweating soldiers staring and silent, and remembers the fight going on in the provinces; the friends this country has taken from her. And there is that odd feeling again that they shouldn't even be here, that this was all a bad idea.

10

Mussulo: December 2006

RUI'S SISTER-IN-LAW, LISETE, slid onto the arm of the couch, smooth thigh against cream leather, placing her drink next to the heavy glass vase overflowing with pink and white lilies, at the beach bar in Mussulo. She sat silently, saying nothing until they were alone, she and Ana. Rui was off shaking hands heartily and being slapped on the back by a man from the government, his wife Joana was calling to her son, asking him if he wanted something to eat and Tiago and Cristina had gone for a walk with the kids. Lisete took the photocopy in her hands. 'I know this woman,' she said. 'I've seen her singing.'

'Are you serious?' Ana asked.

'Yes, for sure. She's older now, much older, but it was definitely the same woman.'

'Where, where did you see her? In one of the clubs here?' Ana was excited, could hardly believe what she was hearing.'

'Oh no,' Lisete responded. 'It wasn't here at all. It was in Paris.'

'Paris?' Ana could feel her face contort. 'Paris?'

'Yes,' Lisete's voice was low. 'I live there.'

'But how could it have been Paris? Where in Paris was it?' Ana asked, becoming aware of the unsteady edge in her tone.

'It was in the Théâtre La Reine Blanche,' Lisete replied. 'Do you know it?'

Ana shook her head, pressed on. 'But was it long ago? When did you see her exactly?'

Lisete thought for a moment. 'It was only about a month ago. Yes, it was the end of November, around the twenty-fifth, some time around my friend Clara's birthday. It was her idea to go.'

Ana took a long drink of her Cutty Sark and Coca-Cola, removed a cigarette from her pack and studied Lisete for a moment through her sunglasses; her full breasts and thick brown hair pulled back from a face that had only the slightest trace of Africa in it, so much lighter than her sister Joana. I wonder if she's really reliable, she thought. Or if she's just got her mixed up with someone else. Surely it couldn't, couldn't have been Solange she saw on that stage in Paris. The other woman seemed to catch on to her appraisal, her judgement of whether she was a fit enough witness to the truth, and feeling caught out Ana looked away. At the glisten of the sun against the shingle, the wooden bridge leading over to the house, lone figure of a man walking its length.

'Her name, her name was Solange, Solange Mendes?' Ana trained her eyes back on Lisete, all moisture leaving her throat, tongue too big and pressed up against the roof of her mouth.

Lisete inhaled on her cigarette. 'Solange, Solange Mendes,' she repeated slowly, name curling into a question mark. 'No, that couldn't have been it. It was something shorter.' There was a pause; 'São,' she clapped her hands together, 'it was just one name, São. I remember because we went with a friend who doesn't speak Portuguese and he asked us if it meant anything or if it was just a name, São. And we told him, told him it meant "saint", like São João. And that it also meant "they". We even pointed to a table of Congolese who were there, said "*Nós somos Angolanas. Eles são Congoleses.*"' Lisete laughed, high-pitched, irritating Ana.

'Then it can't be the same woman I'm looking for,' she confirmed, thinking how silly this Lisete was, sure now the woman she'd seen in Paris didn't have anything to do with Solange. Until it occurred to her that perhaps Lisete had seen the *other* woman in the picture, the one in the *pano*, Solange's cousin. That maybe it was she who'd made it as a singer and Solange was dead, or maybe, just maybe, living here in Angola, all glamour and promise gone to seed in one of the *musseques*.

'Which one was it again?' Ana held out the image once more.

Lisete looked long and hard at it before she answered, 'Yes, it was definitely her,' a sleek nail coated in a clear varnish caressed the woman's neck, travelled the length of her body, along her yellow top and down her jeans. 'She's a bit heavier now, but those eyes, that smile… the same. She was wearing a headscarf, leopard-print, and a long dress when I saw her.'

Ana was puzzled until she thought of another possibility. Maybe the one in the jeans isn't Solange at all, she studied the faces in the picture again. Maybe this other woman isn't a cousin of my mother at all but my actual mother, she stared at the two faces, much younger than hers already. Maybe it *is* the one in the *pano*, the thought raced through her mind.

Not that it was the first time she'd considered this other

body might have been the one she'd begun within. She had wondered, worried, that possibility before, though it was the one in the denims and the headscarf she'd always been instinctively drawn to. Even if there were teenage days when her mind had flip-flopped between both of them, walking through the blue-tiled tunnel beneath the train station or lying on her bed when she got home, trying to summon the energy to get changed out of that damn stupid uniform, attempting to piece it all together, who she was.

Ana noticed that Lisete was looking at her, that it was she who was being studied now, and as their eyes met she saw something in the other woman, some intelligence lurking defensively within her, as well as a certain sensitivity. She pictured a tiny piece of film of Lisete walking around the Jardin du Luxembourg alone, dodging looks that leered, and bitter glances from vacant French women. Just a flicker, a slight quiver, and then her mind returned to the singer. Imagining her suddenly turning up the heat in that room in Paris, raising the stakes, suddenly shuffling her feet, shoulders shimmying and grinning at this crowd of strangers. Heels kicked off as she danced to a semba beat; voice strong, soaring.

Paris, the word rose within her again, an Angolan in Paris walking the city from five to seven before her gig. Winter, late November; bitterly cold, desperately grey, and an African woman moving along the banks of the Seine, red and navy scarf on her head, hoop earrings jangling, breasts moving slightly. With the dark tones of the city so different to Mussulo where everything was bright, white, bleached by the pitiless African sun, this beach bar more like some piece of paradise than a wild corner of another broken dream of a land.

Ana caught sight of Rui walking out of the sea just then,

all slow, bulky masculinity, drops of saltwater caught in the thick, twisted hair of his chest. And felt a flash of a memory of a newspaper photo, small blue swimming trunks, blue eyes, and then something else. Ursula Andress singing, holding a seashell, Sean Connery ready to shake her, stir her, and Rui looking straight at Ana, right at her.

Her eyes fixed again on Lisete, her toned behind heading to the bar now, wondering again exactly what it was she'd seen. Ana imagined the singer performing to pretty girls with their hair in cornrows. Beside good-looking shop-keepers whose skin doesn't shine like petroleum, the way it would back home at this time of year.

And sitting there, alone for a few moments, she put her sunglasses on and resolved to try to contact this woman, this São, to trace her through the Internet as soon as they got back to Luanda the next day. Because if she was a working musician she was sure to have a website, a MySpace page, something. She couldn't be that hard to find. And as soon as she found her, then surely, surely she'd lead her straight to her cousin, to Solange. She was getting closer, wasn't she? Moving definitively closer to Solange.

Who she'd always kept a space safe for, it was true, even if there were times she'd been almost compelled to believe what they never said straight out but sometimes implied, her father and Helena. About how she wasn't fit, wasn't able to be a mother, her real mother, more interested in parties, in music, than taking care of a daughter. But Ana had always known they'd got it wrong, hadn't she? That they didn't know the woman they were talking about. Couldn't know her, not really, because only Ana could, only she had any idea of what she was like… *a minha mãe é linda.*

Though she'd always left her name unsaid, soon as

she was old enough to understand; for shame, for shame, keep your mouth shut. Even if she had nursed a version of the woman's life for decades now, imagining that the real mother and the real Ana were out there somewhere. That was what she'd thought about on empty afternoons down on the beach in Carcavelos, or watching the African women from Marianas, the shanty town in the neighbourhood. *Uazekele kié-uazeka*, her eyes on their ankles, scarves, skirts, their flat noses or fine features, always shifting her upward gaze away before they noticed her, terrified of being caught within their big dark eyes.

But that loyalty towards her mother, that hope that she'd come back for her, had only emerged as rebellion, no, pure resentment, halfway through secondary school. As Ana made accusations against her father and Helena daily. Oh, she'd make them pay, how she'd make them pay, the reckoning had come all right.

She winced inwardly at some of the things she'd said to Helena those years, how she'd faced her down, cool as death, and asked her why she'd raised another woman's child, if she could have been that desperate. Or if she was just using her to make José feel guilty for what he'd done. And that endlessly repeated mantra: 'You're not my real mother. You're not my real mother,' said so often it lost its meaning in the end.

As she watched Lisete chatting at the bar, waiting for the two cocktails, she remembered how her venom had left Helena alone after a time, but had only grown in ferocity and turned her into a monster spitting at her father. Leaving his wife as referee, always attempting to keep the peace, sitting at the kitchen table with her head in her hands, well past midnight, mid-week, wondering how it had all turned out like this.

It was around then she'd begun working on her plants, really taken an interest in them, Helena, bringing them to life when her family was falling to pieces, José and Ana grinding each other down, locked in something she could never really be a part of.

And it was those years, or what had climaxed in those years, that had washed Ana up in Ireland; standing soaked at the airport bus stop that Tuesday afternoon in September, eighteen and wondering if she could survive in this place: dark, dank, dirty, and only early afternoon already. No sky, only charcoal swirls that were smothering her, heart crashing and cursing herself for being so stubborn, so stupid. Close to tears on that stinking, wet homeless dog of a bus headed for Trinity College, the stench of petrol making her stomach revolt.

But somehow, over time, that first clear image of Dublin had receded as she moved inside from out, began to see small, isolated shots. Taking pictures of parks in early November: brown, by red by yellow, golden sunlight. And the Natural History Museum with its Victorian specimens in glass cases, its rickety, narrow staircases. The upstairs of Kehoe's pub off Grafton Street and the bottle-greens and slut-red lipstick tones of window frames and doors against the hushed grey light of December. It had welcomed her, Dublin, hadn't asked who she was, not really, even though the people always wondered. 'Where are you from?' the two women with heavy gold rings and thick accents in the bakery had wondered one day. 'Your hair is gorgeous, love. It's massive. I'd love to have curls like that.'

Yes, it had taken her in, that small, strange city, allowed her to remake herself within its bastardised English, its sullen streets. Revealed its secrets slowly, like a lover she leaned into nightly, hated some mornings. And it had shown her and Helena all of its spring flowers that Saturday afternoon they'd walked from Viking Road to the Botanical Gardens. Most of all its magnolia trees, pink streaks on white satin against the nineteenth-century red-brick houses. In such sudden full flights of life, gone just as quickly.

Luanda: December1967

THERE THEY ARE, ACROSS THE BAY, José and Helena, somewhere between Christmas and New Year, 1967. He wants to go out again, to another party they've been invited to but she says no, thinks they should spend the evening together. 'Let's have some lobster, open that champagne Bruno gave us. We never have any time alone,' weight of the words in her breasts, her behind, her pregnant glances.

Yes, he thinks, she's right. It's hardly ever just the two of them these days. Save for when they're in bed, and even that's changed from the first few months of the honeymoon period. Which took him by surprise somehow, those nights, though he's still not sure why. After all, isn't that what newly-weds do, open one another's bodies up, wet, hard, and that loss of self, that falling into something. A not thinking, not worrying, not trying to put it into place. Sweet obliteration, lay me down, lay me down, but it only lasted so long. Only returns sporadically.

It still exhausts her, the way he has of making life more complicated than it should be, how he thrives on this lack of fulfilment. It's all so draining, watching him wearing himself out, so involved in this shape-shifting drama of his own existence. Lately she can feel him moving away from her: sexually, intellectually. Not that they don't go out together, or make love any more. They do, but something has changed and he's off chasing some unknown again, fired up by the sound and taste and colour of difference, mind spasming with the magic of it all.

He wonders if there is some kind of a pattern for marriage and whether they are following a time-worn trail, Hansel and Gretel. If this is how men feel about their wives after they've taken the plunge. Not really that bothered. But oh, that's harsh, and not even true. He loves Helena, loves her deeply, can't imagine life without her. It's more just, on a day to day level, he isn't always bowled over by the whole situation. If he's honest with himself, that is. Which he is, of course, José de Castro. No truth too big or small. Brave, all-seeing José.

Over a year since the wedding already and it hasn't turned out exactly the way she thought either; worse, better, who can say, all just depends on the day, the way you look at it. But she's still ridiculously fond of him, more than she's ever been of anyone. And that's why she's worried now, afraid he's drifting away. Why it's time to take the relationship in hand, move it on. What this whole night is about really, this languid, apparently unselfconscious stroll from bedroom to bathroom in just a black slip. And the slow rise of the silk above her head, rolling down of her knickers just out of his line of vision as the steam slowly hugs the tiles.

The door to the bathroom remains open. He can't see her but imagines her alabaster buttocks blushing in the steam that brushes against them. Sees himself kneeling behind her, parting her pink lips there on the tiles. Lets the memory of a night pass through him, crouching on that same floor after a few drinks; long, lingering movements of a new way of doing it, hollow of flesh between thumb and index finger, resisting too rapid a release. Drawing it out, telling himself she's asleep anyway, and imagining some other girl, dark brown against white, curtains fluttering and all of the great unknown within her.

She's given up taking the pill, Helena, though she hasn't said anything to him about it. She'll just let him think he's having his wicked way with her, allow him to release himself deep inside her and wait until something starts to grow there, a life they'll make up between them. She's always wanted a baby anyway and after a year it's time; a little sooner than she'd planned but that's okay. If she gets pregnant in the next couple of months, then she'll give birth in early October or November. And it's that life, that new life, that will keep them together.

11

Mussulo: December 2006

ANA WAS LYING ON A WOODEN sun lounger outside Rui's house, abandoned to the morning, hammock empty beside her, strains of the kids squealing on the air. It would be hours before they took the boat back to the city and she turned Tiago's computer on, prayed the connection wouldn't fail, and began to move slowly through pages and more virtual pages, searching for this woman, this São.

Though she wasn't as excited by the prospect as she'd been the day before, the very real possibility that this woman wasn't anything to do with her having slowly taken hold. Maybe neither of the women in the photograph, neither of the cousins, is Solange, she'd got to thinking. After all, nobody had yet confirmed her teenage inclinations. Those two girls in the photograph might just have been other singers from Luanda, one of whom was now performing in Paris, nothing much to do with José. She wondered again if she should have left the picture where she'd found it, all those years ago in Carcavelos.

But still this São might have known Solange, know something of her, Ana tried to put everything in order. Or maybe she really *is* her cousin, maybe you were right yesterday, her mind flipped backwards and she felt the hope rising inside her. She looked out at the water again and thought of *Tabu*, all the South Sea islanders moving in their boats across Murnau's film. Then ran her hand along the cover of her book on post-classical Hollywood cinema, thinking she should really get on with reading it. Though all she felt like doing now was lying here, with her long limbs laid out.

So much time spent reading, pushing, learning, doing the impossible. 'You have to learn to relax, to make time for yourself,' the words of a friend late one Friday afternoon in November, the Liffey suddenly magnified, grey and fast-moving below her apartment on Parliament Street. At least the rings beneath my eyes are receding, Ana thought. Maybe they'll even disappear completely one day if I give up smoking. She lit a cigarette, leaned back and let the sweet smoke fill up her lungs.

Looked down at her bright orange bikini, gaze resting on her stomach, wondering if she'd lost weight or gained weight over the last couple of weeks. I'd better not forget to take my malaria tablet again, she reminded herself, thinking of her slip the day before and the story about the local whose body had bloated with the disease. Her skin was changing colour, wasn't it? No longer the dishcloth tone it had turned in winter. Her eyes moved over to Rui fixing something outside the wooden house, then back to her stomach.

Yes, it's definitely darker, she could almost see it turning a shade before her tired eyes, thought how she no longer minded watching it. Even enjoyed it sometimes, this metamorphosis, this emergence of the real Ana, or an image of her anyway, the one that might have been. She inhaled again, remembering herself in Lanzarote one February afternoon, so dark inside the cool apartment after the over-exposed white light by the pool. Standing naked in front of the mirror, looking at her brown skin and the pale stains of breasts and buttocks, running her hands over her body and wondering that this was her, was Ana, falling back onto the cool white sheets of the bed, fingers moving in a slow hunger.

Like last night with Lisete, hands and tongue following the curves of her beautiful body, moving into her. Gone back to Luanda early this morning, Lisete, then off to Namibe with her mother. She wondered if that was why Rui was so quiet now, because his sister-in-law had got to Ana first. In another life, on another day, she might have had him instead, as well, but it was Lisete she'd enjoyed herself with the night before.

Her gaze moved on, over to the city, which hovered hazily across the water in the distance, before she closed her eyes, recalling herself as a child and how she'd adored the beach then. Playing for hours down by St Julian's Fort, long Sundays over at Costa da Caparica with fish and chips afterwards, the smoky smell of sardines grilling outside. Or watching the ships coming and going from new places that she would make it her business to find out something about, heaving the big slabs of encyclopaedias down from the white bookshelves at home, tracing her fingers along maps and photographs of American Indian faces. She'd wandered the sands of Carcavelos even in winter, blown from one end of the beach to the other, thinking how sad and desperate the fading paint of the restaurants closed for the season seemed, calculating how long it would be before she could slip back into the water.

The Little Mermaid, that was what Helena had called her, for that story book seemed to be wedged under her arm for a few months one year. She could still see her, the little mermaid, swimming up to the surface of the water that first time, to see how they lived on the other side. And even now, as an adult, it could trouble her sometimes, that trading of a fin for legs, and how she sacrificed her voice to the sea witch, all for the prospect of walking on dry land.

They took it from her, the beach, that was all there was to it, Ana told herself again. Oh, she didn't believe that lives were just made up of momentous moments, always thought that things gathered space, weight, life, beneath surfaces, beneath time, that they didn't just happen the way people led you to believe, but sometimes, sometimes... Yes, that afternoon had changed her, taken the beach from her. Cut down to half her size over the course of a couple of hours.

They'd gone to the big outdoor swimming pool, the Piscina Oceânica de Oireas, that was where it had all begun. But no, it was before that, at the tip of a tail end of that first secondary-school year when she'd begun palling around with Susana and Louise, when they had suddenly, unaccountably, begun courting her friendship. Susana with that sleek black hair she was always pulling across her face, and Louise with her squeaky-clean white tennis shoes and English mother. Never could quite get what anybody saw in Louise, all cold bones and disinfected beauty, like Olivia Newton John in *Grease* put through a slow wash. But anyway they were her friends, were friendly, and Ana was glad to have them. To not have to work so hard just to get people to give her the time of day.

Even though that was all it became in the end, hard work. Pretending she liked Bryan Adams when she was getting down to The Stones, The Byrds, other LPs she'd slide from her father's collection and take to her room. And she didn't even protest the odd joke they made about her out of nowhere. Took it on the chin and let Susana put her arm around her shoulder, saying that's all it had been, a joke. It seemed to be what was involved in being part of a gang, and everybody knew that having a place in one was a marker of your worth, your youth. And once she'd begun sloping around the little shopping centre near her apartment, smoking cigarettes and sitting moodily in the park with them, it felt like life had always been like this. Like these hot, arid days of late July, well into the summer holidays already, time sitting still, the girls growing like wallflowers.

'Let's go to the *Piscina Oceânica*,' Susana said out of nowhere one Thursday afternoon.

'Yeah, cool, let's go,' Ana cheered, wondering why it was she and not Louise who'd said something. Because that was the way it worked, wasn't it? Always Susana or Louise who spoke first, Ana mumbling something at the end that they didn't really bother to listen to, inane add-ons that they were right to discard. Just the hierarchy of the small group, the way it worked, and she was only a blow-in anyway, knew her place.

'All right, I'll see if I can get some money from my mother,' Louise said, 'meet me at the station in an hour.' Before the obligatory hugs they traded every time they met and said goodbye.

It must have been six, or half-past six, when they opened the top level of the concrete diving board. Evening anyway, when they let the teenagers climb all the way up there and fling themselves into the blue seawater below. And Ana was a good swimmer, a strong swimmer, had been moving through water since she was a baby. It was just that she wasn't too crazy about heights. But as Susana and Louise watched a group of boys the year ahead of them at St Julian's make a big show of hurling themselves down into the water, one of them, or both of them, decided they'd show them they'd met their match, climbing the steps already.

But the cement only felt rough, uncomfortable, under Ana's feet as she began her ascent, noticing people watching their climb, all the sunbathers laid out like strips of sizzling meat along the tiers around the pool. And when they reached, finally reached the top, she felt ready to vomit, peering around her like a newborn kitten, the 25 de Abril Bridge down towards the city and the Christ the King statue across the water.

Susana went first, perched on the edge, drawing the moment out, before she executed a perfect dive, the rowdy boys cheering as she hit the surface of the water that swallowed her up. Before one, two, all of them looked up again, shouting for Louise to jump. Slowly she moved out, but she looked back at Ana as she did so, suddenly afraid, really afraid, as if she was pleading with her, asking her to protect her, to prevent her from doing this. Yet all Ana could think was that as soon as Louise jumped it would be her turn, that she'd no longer be able to hide behind time or other people. Louise threw her a sudden look of contempt, then shrugged her apprehension off in one great surge of courage and leaped away from safety, arms straight above her head.

Ana stepped out quickly, listening to the boys whistle and shout their approval at Louise, moving to the spot where her friend had stood, trying to make her mind go blank. But as soon as she looked down she could feel her legs and chest weakening, could see Louise and Susana standing in the pool with the boys, all in a great huddle, and feel herself up there alone. She allowed herself to imagine going back, inching her way away from the edge but knew she couldn't dare go running, screaming, shaking, shivering back to earth. 'I have to jump, have to jump.'

They began to clap, slowly, rhythmically. 'Hurry up,' shouted one of the boys. 'Get a move on,' another and then somebody else said something clever, something she couldn't make out, but the others laughed loudly. Ridiculous, awkward, that's how she thought she must look, as she heard a lone voice calling up, '*Vem, bastarda, vem!*' Everything stopped.

It was Louise and that word spat at her once, was it once or twice before, back in the early days, then never mentioned again because of how silent Ana had turned. But there it was again, out of nowhere, a secret weapon, a wallop on her face. '*Vem, bastarda, vem!*' they were all soon chanting, before she had time to fully take in what was happening, wondering if the boys really knew what they were saying. But she felt sure Susana and Louise did, while all the sunbathers wearing headphones simply looked on and smiled because to them it was just a group of girls playing in the sun. How could they know what they were doing to her up there, her friends, the bitches?

She fell out into the air. Slowly, slowly down until her body met the water with a crash, chest aching and arms flailing as she struggled towards the surface, wondering how she was going to face Susana and Louise, what she would say, and how anything would ever be the same after this.

Bastarda, such a stupid fucking joke, she thought as she swam to the side of the pool, got out, grabbed her bag and headed for the dressing room. Feeling sure the other two were staring open-mouthed at her jerky movements, shocked at her assertiveness. But she didn't give a damn what they thought.

And as she caught sight of herself in the mirror inside she knew exactly why they'd said what they had – because her skin was dark, getting much darker, and it was obvious José and Helena couldn't both be her biological parents. That suddenly seemed so clear as she dried herself carelessly, pulled her underwear, denim shorts and T-shirt on, slotted the flip-flops between her toes.

And as she began the long walk back to the train station, she only wished none of this had happened. That they were still lying in the sun, looking up at the diving board and its top level that wouldn't be opened that day. Because if it was still a few hours before then she'd be safe. Instead now she'd have to keep away from the pool for the rest of the summer, and put a distance between herself and the beach, watching her back every time she passed the shopping centre, for fear Susana and Louise were following her, making fun of her again. Or, worst of all, trying to make amends.

So much holiday still to go and all that was left was for her to make a space, a place, at home in the apartment where she could try and block everything out. Making sure Tiago, her father and Helena didn't find out what was wrong with her. But eventually, eventually she'd have to go back to school; she couldn't even bear to think about late August. Why did this happen? a desolate voice in her head and that very first flinch of fingernails along the inside of her arm, her long, lone silhouette moving along beside her, and still such a long way to go.

Luanda: May 1968

WARM EVENING, LATE MAY, screen vast, and seemingly thousands of chairs already filled. Helena looks, eyes beady, for their seats, all in a tizzy, cursing José for being late again, for making her rush like this. Silently blaming him now because she's given up chastising him for the night. Sitting beside him in the car, fixing the hem of her dress, asking him, 'Why can't you be on time, just once? It doesn't matter what pullover you wear if you can't see the reflection of your face in your shoes.' But he doesn't listen, never does, José. Lounging in different positions on the sofa, listening to events unfolding in Paris on the radio, then jolting out of his imagination at the very last moment and scrambling to get ready. Though he doesn't just throw his keys in his pocket, sports jacket over his shoulder, oh no. Has to wash his face and under his arms first, find a pressed shirt, go to the toilet. Telling her, cool as a cucumber, '*Calma, calma*, we have enough time.'

He notices an enormous sign, a girl in a bathing suit drinking a beer, then looks down towards the water, the ships going and coming. Thinks of all those millions rounded up, rammed onto vessels and taken away through Luanda.

The end, the beginning, of a vast slave route, all along the River Kuanza. So many dying on the way, the journey across the water a death even for those who survived, born again over there in São Salvador, in Rio, *semba* beats miraculously finding life again. It astounds him sometimes, this capacity for survival. And fascinates him, it's true, sets him all aspin, the thought of those beats on the waves and that new culture, music, world, rising up from the blood, the broken… He thinks of the guerrillas fighting in the countryside, wonders if Lisbon will ever give up the colonies. What would happen to Helena and me then? he ponders, but puts negative prospects aside.

Because she's found two seats, Helena. They're not theirs but anyway the film is starting, some other couple must have taken theirs, oh and who knows if anybody even pays any attention to the seat numbers on the tickets. *The Graduate*, it was her choice, this American film, looked like the best on offer, a young, unknown actor walking by a wall, but she isn't in the mood now to watch it, or not with José anyway. He's only making her calculate everything she can't stand about him, as he sits there taking up so much space, so engrossed in the film already. She moves slightly away from him, plays with the gold hem of her new dress again.

I'm doing my best, I'm trying, he tells himself. He knows she wants this baby, that she's been attempting to get pregnant since Christmas. Would have known even if she hadn't brought it up when things weren't going as quickly as she had hoped, planned. And he might have thought her sly, underhand, skin serenading him into bed for some other purpose than the momentary pleasure of it, only it isn't his style. He tends to go along with things, to trust she knows what she's doing, knows how to hold them together. Thank

God one of them does.

Her breathing slowly steadies and she stops wanting to kill him, but just as soon as she relaxes into her seat her stomach turns at the thought that she is behaving like her mother, turning right into the woman. She shifts her cardigan slightly, enjoying the feel of the soft yellow wool on her neck, then pushes a strand of hair back into her bun and wonders if she's really, really going to do it. Mrs Robinson! Yes, yes she is, she's taking her dress off right in front of Benjamin. And she'll get him in the end, what she wants from him! So many nights Helena has carried out her own little seductions, not usually as upfront as this but slowly working on making him want her. God, it's boring sometimes, the old routine. But she wants this baby, should be pregnant by now, will give it another couple of months before she goes to the doctor.

He puts his hand in hers, gentle, and she feels a shiver along her skin, out of nowhere, with the thought of a night a few weeks ago when it was true, they really did make love. Both of them unthinking and slow, hard movements, a long sleep afterwards.

And as he caresses her hand, he senses a flutter in his stomach. Thinks yes, they'll make love tonight, lay limbs coiled into the next morning and then make it again if they feel like it. Odd, isn't it, that this mood sometimes takes him out of nowhere, galloping ahead of thoughts and doubts, as if none of that mattered? Yes, they'll have a drink, then head for the bedroom. And he'll let down her hair and run his tongue along her neck, pressed into her, beauty.

12

Luanda: December 2006

MYSPACE, ANA THOUGHT she might as well start there. She didn't have a profile herself, but friends from Dublin, some of whom were musicians, some just wanting a bit of attention, used it. 'São,' she put the name in and clicked on the search button, then watched as young men from California and women from Japan appeared. Hundreds, there were hundreds of people by the name of São using the site. She trawled through the first couple of pages, hitting one profile, then another, taken into pages of people's lives; looking at interests, photographs, thank you notes. It all seemed so odd somehow.

And fascinating, in a morbid sort of way; she could have gone on like this all evening really, but forced herself to focus, told herself her São had to be there somewhere. She moved back to the homepage, saw that she could search under musical artists, and entered the name again. Still hundreds of entries: jazz singers in Switzerland, rock groups from Brazil, pianists from France... but yes, there she was. Ana opened the page up. It was her, of course it was her.

São: *Semba*. Location – Luanda, Paris. Profile views – 68,751. Last login – 23/12/2006. There were photos, a video too. Ana paused for a moment, hand on her forehead, before she went into the pictures. And there she was again, São, in a floor-length pink dress that tied around the neck, a pattern of printed flowers and leaves spilling down its front. Another shot where she was wearing a dark green silk dress. Then another in a yellow *pano*, with a colourful pattern running through it. Ana looked at her face; her eyes, her lips.

Stayed staring at the photographs a few long minutes before going back to the woman's profile. Where she saw there was a list of upcoming concerts. 'Luanda, The Kilamba Cultural Centre, Friday 12 January 2007,' Ana read out loud. Shit, that's the day I'm going home, she remembered and felt her hope thud to a stop, wondering if there was any way to change her departure date.

The Kilamba Cultural Centre, she read the name again, thinking it sounded familiar, before she remembered it was Luísa who'd mentioned it. Who'd said she was singing there on New Year's Eve, that Ana should come along. Well, if this São is in Angola now, then surely she'll be there that night, Ana reasoned. And if she is then I'll be able to find her, ask her if she is Solange's cousin, if she knows anything about her.

She scrolled up the page, to the recordings of the woman singing, then clicked play on the first of these, a track called 'Mulemba', determined to send her a message now, wondering what she'd write. Only she'd have to create a profile for herself if she was to do that, she remembered. 'Tiago, Tiago,' she began to call, only then realising he was standing right there, at the door, listening to the song.

When they got to the Kilamba Cultural Centre on New Year's Eve the place was already full of musicians. Older, of course, than during their glory days. Ana smiled at men her father's age and more: slouching, receding, greying, slowing, slapping hands, holding their stomachs and chortling. One of them grinned back as he passed, big white teeth, cotton-wool hair, taking in her long silhouette, canary yellow dress stretching right to the ground.

She looked up at the sky, then out at the crowd, thinking I'm looking good, looking good tonight, noticing other glances, both furtive and open, from women in the audience. Who were either dressed in traditional *panos*, like the fancy crinkled pink one the tall woman wore, or smart dresses, hair newly done, skin shimmering. Do I have too much bone on show though? Ana asked herself, looking down at the neckline that went almost as far as the thick black belt clasped around her tiny waist. Not that there's all that much to exhibit compared to some here, she glanced at a pair of heavy breasts that looked set to break for the border any minute. I wonder what will happen if she gets up to dance, she could already see a couple of guys with greedy eyes shaking their hips around the woman, looks passing from her breasts to her enormous backside.

'Luísa,' the woman seemed to materialise out of nowhere, wrapped in layers of fabric, white polka dots on red, head-scarf the same pattern. Ana leaned in to kiss her, noticing the red lipstick, the violet eyeshadow. 'Ó Ana, you're here?' Luísa seemed surprised and glad she'd made it.

'Of course. It was a bit of an escapade trying to get a ticket but Tiago managed. You haven't met my brother, have you?' Tiago was coming back from the bar, a *caipirinha* in each hand, never one to waste any time getting into the swing of a night out.

'*Olá*,' he kissed Luísa on both cheeks, 'a pleasure to meet you.'

'Yes, you too,' she looked closely at Tiago. 'You have the same eyes as your sister.'

'Oh yeah? Must be our father,' he replied, Ana watching his hazel eyes, thinking it was true.

'Would you like a drink, Luísa?' he asked, but somebody, a man in cream slacks, shirt open at the collar, straw hat on his head, had come up to the woman, was busy hugging her, saying something in Kimbundu both Tiago and Ana missed.

'Are you sure Cristina is okay staying in?' she asked again as her eyes scanned the crowd.

'Yeah, don't worry,' Tiago answered. 'She doesn't like New Year's Eve, never has. Not even when we were living in Portugal. Thinks it's a load of hype.'

'Just the two of us then,' Ana smiled, a vision of Tiago rolling up a note for her in the toilet of a bar in Bairro Alto, the two of them later walking to Belém train station at seven in the morning, somehow ending up in photos taken by some Chinese tourists. 'Nearly a year already,' she shook her head, remembering the great escape they'd made a few nights after Helena's funeral. Running off to party in Lisbon, just like old times.

'Excuse me, I have to go now, but see you after the show,' Luísa walked off, still chatting loudly with the man, leaving Ana regretting she hadn't told her about her new lead, about the concert Lisete had seen in Paris, about the message she'd sent to São.

'What time is she on at?' Tiago asked, looking up at the musicians who'd started their set.

'I don't know,' Ana answered, 'She's just doing a few songs.'

'*Olha*, there's Artur,' Tiago pointed out a tall man over

to the left. Not bad-looking, thought Ana as they went over to his table, beaming a big smile down on him, taking him by surprise.

'I'm Artur,' he shook her hand, kissed her gently. 'You're Tiago's sister, right? What's your name?'

'Ana,' she answered, 'I'm Ana,' bending over to plant a kiss on his wife's cheek.

'I'm Paula,' there was a full smile, not a care in the world. 'Sit down, please sit down.'

Ana pulled out a chair, lifted the hem of her dress as Tiago and Artur drifted off to talk to another friend. 'What brings you here tonight?' Paula seemed to take all of Ana in quickly.

'Oh, I met one of the singers last week and she said it might be a good night,' she responded, then thought of something. 'You don't, by any chance, know a singer, an Angolan singer called São?' she asked quickly.

'No. No I don't,' Paula answered, 'why do you want to know?'

'Oh, it's nothing,' said Ana, feeling suddenly foolish for blurting out the inquiry.

'Are you from Luanda?' she changed the subject.

'Yes, Luanda,' Paula confirmed. 'And you? You live in Lisbon, do you, Ana?'

'Lisbon, no,' she replied, her eyes scouring the crowd again, 'I haven't lived in Lisbon in more than ten years.'

'Don't you like it there?' Paula came out with another question.

'Yes, yes. I go there a few times a year. My father is still living there, but I wouldn't fancy it. Tut, tut, tut,' Ana wondered again when this tongue clicking had started, if she'd just absorbed it by osmosis.

Then remembered, out of nowhere, that she nearly *had* moved back to Portugal once. Just after she'd finished her philosophy and English degree at Trinity. Almost, so nearly, seduced by Lisbon that summer, the city unfolding itself before her in the afternoon heat; its ragged splendour and her fantasies of times past, running fingers along the tiles of old buildings, their endless designs and that taste of the possibility of a return. No longer even afraid to go down to the beach, laying her sarong out when it was quiet in the mornings, eating hamburgers in the wooden restaurant down by the tower and listening to the sounds of different languages all around her.

'And you, do you like living in Luanda, Paula?'

'*Sim*, I like it,' Paula replied. It's very cosmopolitan, you know. But it gets crazy sometimes. So chaotic, so much *confusão*. It's nice to get away sometimes, to Namibia, to South Africa. Have you been to Namibia?'

'No,' Ana shook her head, picturing desert beaches, the enormous bones of long dead animals, before her mind flipped back to Lisbon, to what she felt about it.

And how she'd steeled herself against the place, fought those feelings emerging inside her as June turned. Walking up Rua do Alecrim slowly, towards Largo de Camões, where everybody in Lisbon passes sooner or later, memories trickling back with the beat of the sun on her forehead, scent of the breeze coming up off the river. Thinking of those Saturday afternoons with her *Tia* Isabel, her aunt who lived in New York City, their special days together once every six months when she was back in Portugal. Floating through the streets of the Baixa, the Chiado, searching out shoes and gloves, lipsticks and face powder, books and old maps of old Lisbon town. Isabel, still striking, strong, streak of silver running right through her hair. And hadn't known, that summer, how she'd spend the following one with her in New York, out in Jackson Heights.

'Have you been enjoying the nightlife?' Artur seemed to appear again out of nowhere, pulled Ana from the past and put another *caipirinha* in front of her, something else, a rum and Coca-Cola maybe, before Paula. She nodded. 'Have you been out dancing?'

'Dancing around the apartment,' Tiago laughed, 'We're stay-at-homers now, what with the girls and everything.'

'Eh, maybe Cristina, but not you, Tiago,' Paula wore a look of scepticism for a long moment.

'Oh no, that's not true. I'm a modern kind of guy,' Tiago responded, 'not like the men in the old days.'

'I'll bet,' Paula held her look. 'And when was the last time you changed a nappy?'

'Eh, I change myself every day, isn't that enough?'

'*Olha*, Paula, leave the man alone, *eh pá!*' Artur chided.

'Oh, I'd say *you* do everything at home yourself,' Ana accused her brother's friend. 'I can just see you preparing the rice for dinner.'

'You haven't tasted my cooking yet, lady, you just wait and see,' he answered back.

'Is that a threat or a promise?' Ana laughed.

And she was still laughing an hour or so later as she pulled Tiago up to dance, the blare of brass startling them as an older man came out on stage. Tiago put his left hand on her lower back, holding her right arm up, and then they were off, round in moody circles. While Artur moved, legs like elastic, next to the chair where Paula was still sitting, laughing out loud and clapping her hands. As Ana began thinking she hadn't enjoyed herself like this for a while now:

good drink, good music to dance to, the singer over sixty but still grooving, hip-shimmying, in his brightly-coloured shirt.

She remembered São then and looked around again for any sign of her, thinking how this woman would be performing on the stage before them in a couple of weeks. Maybe I should try to speak to Luísa again later, she thought, get her to ask around. Though for now all she wanted was to carry on dancing, snake-hip the night into one to be remembered, as the band went into another tune and she moved back from Tiago and into the beat of the drums, the guitar, the music.

Luanda: February 1969

HEAT RISING, MID-FEBRUARY. Helena is at home, alone, early on a Saturday afternoon, thinking she should really tidy the place up. There are breakfast dishes still in the sink, newspapers and books all over the table, and a couple of stray socks on the floor. She could water the plants too, but she doesn't know where to begin really, feels exhausted already. She goes to the bedroom, runs her hands along the tiny babygrows, lifts them to her face; can almost smell her child already.

While he's at a café not far from home, José, interviewing an older writer for a feature he's doing for a South African newspaper. Which may even make it all the way to London, who knows? And he's asking him about Angolan writers putting the *musseques* on the literary map, giving the people a voice, a presence, bringing them into the written world. He'd like to write himself too, José, but thinks he'll learn all he can from his job first. And that's going well too; he's actually working as the editor of a novel for the first time now.

Funnily enough Helena is thinking about these new Angolan novels too. About how so many people in the *musseques* can't even read or write, can't recognise themselves in these words because they don't make sense to them. Strange coded symbols huddled together like families, that's what they must seem like, she thinks to herself as she puts a book back on the shelf.

And it's then it first hits her, the savage pain between her legs. She can feel it, her waters breaking, oozing down between her thighs. She puts her hand there but there's a lot of it, sticky and heavy, and it's blood. The pain knocks her back onto the sofa.

José shakes the man's hand and looks after him as he walks away, wondering how he has arrived at this point in his life. What makes a writer a writer, a man a man. Before he puts his sunglasses on and heads for home, thinking he'll take Helena for a spin to the Iha. Maybe they can have lunch at a restaurant there, or a picnic. He notices the bakery on his left.

'Good afternoon,' the owner greets him, 'everything good? How is Helena?'

'Good, yes, everything is fine.'

'How long to go now?' she asks.

'Just over a month,' he replies, 'though they say they often go late on their first, isn't that right?'

'*Sim*, senhor, but I was late on all three of mine. Boy or girl, what do you think it will be?'

'A boy, definitely a boy,' he smiles as he pays, takes the small box of cakes and walks out, then gets distracted and finds himself inside a record shop.

Where is he? Where the hell is he? Helena asks herself, thinking she has to get up, find some way to get to the hospital and help her little baby out. Her girl, it's going to be a girl, isn't it? the thought heaves through her. She's always wanted a girl, never had a sister at home. But once it's healthy, that's all that matters, the terrible prospect of something really bad happening hits her. Why isn't he here, never here when I need him? A twist of agony as she lifts herself slowly up, taking in the blood-soaked sofa as she goes slowly to the neighbours to ask for help.

And it's they who tell José, or the wife Rita anyway, when he eventually returns, that she's gone, Helena. That Fragata has taken her to the hospital.

13

Luanda: January 2007

ANA LOOKED DOWN AT THE CITY: the cranes, the TV aerials tangled up in the morning sky, the roofs of unkempt white buildings, each different to the next, all leading down to the ocean. And thought of Tel Aviv, Cairo, places she had never been, urban roofscapes by warm seawaters. She considered maybe there was a kind of sense to what she was seeing, a kind of beauty to it when looked at from here, taken as a whole. Jean Gabin scaling the Kasbah roofs: *Pépé le Moko*.

She ran a hand along the orange silk of her dressing gown as she watched another scene coming into focus, a tracking shot of a city from a height and a woman smoking above it, out on a ledge. What was that film? Where was it from? Turkey? Kazakhstan? No, Georgia. *Since Otar Left*, the English title seemed to steal into her mind, set off a delicious release through her body. Before more scenes began moving behind her eyes: the grandmother in her garden, the platform of a metro station in Tbilisi, the granddaughter behind the glass at Charles de Gaulle Airport.

And that scene in the sitting room, when the family break into spontaneous song and the mother begins to dance with her boyfriend. Ana could remember the small shock of it even now, the life there, the vitality, the tears coming in a rush to her eyes in the almost empty cinema.

She lit another cigarette and wondered if she was ever going to find her mother, if this São had just been another dead end. She'd been so certain, so sure of seeing her at the concert in the Kilamba Cultural Centre, but in the end it had come to nothing. Well anyway, it was a good night, a great night, she sighed, then smiled at the image of Tiago rooted to the spot, shaking his body, dancing Angolan style, the way he'd done as a kid.

Ana heard the door open then, turned around and began to smile, but the look on her brother's face made her stop. He handed her the phone. '*Estou?*' she put it to her ear. 'Ana? Is that Ana?' the voice seemed abrupt, almost aggressive.

'*Sim*, I'm Ana,' she answered coldly.

'Ó Ana, it's really you?' the voice softened, became light, sweet, searching for confirmation.

'Yes, it's me,' she replied, understanding suddenly who this was, and thinking what a fool she was for not realising immediately. 'São, São, is that you?'

'Yes it's me, daughter. It's me. I got your message. But call me Solange. Oh daughter… '

'But what… I sent that message to São. Is she your cousin? Did she tell you? What…'

'Cousin? No, it's me. São is just a name I use for singing,' the voice trembled down the line as Ana stood there in silence, still looking out over the city, but registering almost nothing now.

She realised she should say something. 'Are…?'

But the woman had started speaking again. '*Desculpe*, I just saw your message this morning. Oscar said I should try,

try and see if it was you. Oh, can it really be you, Ana? After all this time, all these years?'

Ana felt the tears come, fought them back. 'Yes, it's me, really me. And it's you... Solange? Can we meet, when can we meet?' She didn't know what to say, just blurted out the question, as if drugged by this sudden, mad hunger to see the woman.

'Tomorrow?' the voice asked.

'Yes, tomorrow, tomorrow,' Ana was excited.

'Okay. At four,' she said. 'We can meet in a lovely bar I know, it's in a garden. I can SMS you the name and address later.'

'Of course, of course,' Ana agreed.

'I can't believe you're here, Ana. Are you with José, is José with you?'

The question made Ana freeze. 'No, he's not here,' she answered, flash of steel rising in her voice.

'But he's still alive?'

'Yes, he's still alive, in Lisbon,' she replied neutrally. Then almost, almost said, But Helena's dead, she died last year, remembering they had started into another year already, stopping just before the first word. 'I'm staying with Tiago. He's living here now.'

'Tiago, little Tiago is living back here?' she sounded surprised.

'Yes, yes, he's been here for years, ' Ana forced some warmth into her voice.

'Tut, tut, tut, tut, tut, and I never had any idea.'

Ana started to speak again, but Solange got there first. 'And you, Ana? What about you? Tell me about yourself,' she was saying.

'Me? I live in Ireland now, in Dublin. I teach film,' she

answered, though really she didn't know what to say, somehow frightened, wary, holding back. 'But let's talk properly tomorrow,' she proposed quickly. 'Four o'clock, no?'

'*Sim*, four o' clock,' Solange confirmed, went quiet for a moment. 'You'll be there, Ana, won't you?'

Ana noticed how close to cracking the voice seemed, felt her own begin to falter. 'Yes, I'll be there,' she managed, suddenly desperate to be alone, in silence, so she could comprehend what was going on, understand how she felt. '*Adeus*.'

'*Adeus*, Ana.'

Luanda: April 1969

THE HEAT NEVER SEEMS TO RELENT at this time of year. Four o'clock in the morning and already she has to turn on the fan in the corner. She clicks the cream glass lamp on as well and wonders if she can get away with playing the radio very low. Turns the dial of the brown transistor to a station that runs through the night and sits back into the sofa as classical tunes breathe into the room. The weak glow from the lamp leaves half her face in shadow, illuminates the other half, and brings out the violence of her hair colour. So much shorter since she decided on a whim to have it cut one afternoon, such a relief to be rid of it in this rising heat, and such a shock for José, the boyish cut. 'What have you done to your hair?'

A boy. She hums along and looks down into the sleepy, bright eyes, takes her breast out and moves the baby's mouth so it can suck. There's a small, sharp pain but she doesn't mind; it's just another proof, another manifestation, of what they share. So odd to think of life without Tiago now, can barely remember what her days were like before she had him, what she did with all her time. Because there's none now, not a free minute to run to the shops, to read a book, to sew the green skirt hanging in the wardrobe. Not that she's complaining, even if she is worn out, even if it seems as though she's sleepwalking day and night. She's never known love like this.

He was sure it would be a boy, José; knew they would call him after his own father, and that he would be just perfect. But what he didn't expect was how this little bundle of flesh would take Helena from him so completely. How sometimes it would seem as though she'd fallen in love with somebody else, was having another relationship right under his roof, both parties complicit in the liaison and acting as if he didn't exist. Sometimes he sits and watches Helena become a mother and sometimes he misses her terribly. Or feels as though he's a clumsy ghost in the wings. But he tries not to dwell on it, sleeps through until six, then goes into the city and attempts to make himself meaningful.

But she has a child, a real child to take care of now, Helena. Is too busy looking after Tiago to even think about José. Who's about as useful as ever, sitting on the side-lines, watching life drifting by, apparently unaware of how things get done: how the baby stays alive and the world keeps turning. Oh, maybe that isn't true. After all he does sheepishly offer to help sometimes. But his version of help always seems to make things more complicated. No, what she's focused on now is Tiago, José will just have to wait. Let him sleep.

Though there have been nights, more than one, when he hasn't been able to sleep at all. Has just lain awake beneath the bright reds and blues of the print above the bed, listening to the sound of her sandals padding the floor, his head on the pillow and despair rising as he sees himself coming home with the stupid box of cakes that morning. Smiling like a fool at Rita, feeling fantastic after the interview, glad the pressure is off and beginning to plan his introduction. Noticing his own face fall as she tells him the news, cursing himself already for not being there.

Even though that wouldn't have changed anything, wouldn't have made a difference, that's what the doctor said. But he still wonders if it has come between himself and Helena. Thinks there's another sin to add to the list, more guilt to twist in his side.

It's at odd moments – walking in the park on a cloud-less day when the sky is pale blue and enormous, or as she's making the dinner, Tiago asleep in his basket – that it hits Helena. Still seems like something that shouldn't have any-thing to do with her, she thinks now as she listens to the screeches of two cats making love, wondering if she should change the yellow curtains. She recalls in a rush the wild pain that morning and all the blood, never thought there could have been so much inside her. 'I'm afraid, Senhora de Castro, that you won't be able to have any more children,' that's what he said, the doctor, as if it was an unambiguous fact, no way around it. 'We're just lucky we saved this one,' looking like he wanted to pat himself on the back. Even though it was she who'd saved her child, only she could have done that.

14

Luanda: January 2007

'FUCK,' ANA MUTTERED as she stood under the shower and realised with a horrible certainty that the water had been cut off. And it had been working earlier, just an hour before, when she'd lathered up her hair, then washed the shampoo out and combed the conditioner slowly through it. Why didn't you have your shower, just finish your hair then? she accused, fury rising, running her nails quickly along her arm. She looked at herself in the mirror, eyes faded and the frown lines along her forehead settling in for the long haul. Then cursed herself again for going to the Portuguese café a few streets away, letting the chestnut conditioner soak in, wanting everything to be perfect for her first meeting with her mother.

Four o'clock, that was when they had arranged to meet. Where, she wasn't sure, but Tiago said he knew the place all right, knew it well. But that was no excuse for her sitting in the café, just an hour before the appointed time, returning loaded glances from interested Lebanese men and drinking another coffee, instead of getting herself ready to meet her mother.

But my outfit is ironed already and I have time, plenty

of time, Ana remembered thinking those exact words in the café as she stood in the bathroom now, putting her dress back on over her head. So strange, how certain she'd been, but she'd lingered too long over her coffee, then walked to Tiago's place like she didn't have a care in the world, swinging her arms and clicking her fingers as she went. And now the water was off she'd never make it in time to meet her mother. She opened the door and called out to her brother, hiding her harassment and lowering her tone only at the last moment. 'Tiago, there isn't any water. Do you know what I can do?'

He knew better than to make a joke, but usually he would have at least smiled to himself at what a disaster this would be for her. He'd been quiet, so quiet though, since he'd passed the phone to her the afternoon before. 'We can use the water in the barrel in the kitchen,' he said. 'Will cold do or do you want me to heat it up on the cooker?'

'No, cold is fine,' she called out, bracing herself for the icy chill of it.

While Tiago fetched the water she went and looked at her jumpsuit laid out on Carolina's bed, feeling suddenly certain that there was no way she could wear it, that the colours were just too bright and it would overpower Solange. Shit, she'd changed her mind about the clothes she'd meet her mother in so often over the years, and then late last night she'd chosen this, finally settled on this flared jumpsuit. Now though, it only served to frustrate her, lying stupidly there on the bed, conspiring against her like everything else on this day that should have been just right. She opened the wardrobe, running item after item of clothing through her mind, then pushing them aside on their hangers. No, there's nothing here, nothing here. I've nothing to wear, she put her fingers to her hair and pulled.

Then made herself sit down on the bed and take a few deep breaths before she walked back over to the wardrobe and in a couple of shrewd moves put another look together: a knee-length fifties dress, patterns of green flowers on white, plastic beaded detail around its neckline. A little green bolero jacket to wear over it. Just light enough to get away with in this heat, she thought to herself, then crouched down and took her tan peep-toe heels from under the bed. Perfect, and I can wear the red sunglasses as well, she cheered up suddenly, then thought of the blonde woman she'd seen in the café, the soft French roll of her hair, and remembered she'd have to put her own up into a bun now to go with these clothes.

Damn, she thought, that will take more time to do. Another five minutes at least, she guessed as she went to see if the water was ready. She began to curse herself again, then slowed down, suddenly asking herself why she was in such a rush anyway, getting herself in such a tizzy to be on time; to be presentable, to be the daughter this woman had never had. She's kept me waiting long enough, the voice in her head was clear, cold, but as soon as the thought came to her she imagined her mother, Solange, this woman, waiting alone in the bar, then getting up and slapping her face when she finally arrived because this was no way to treat her. She shivered, whether at the indignity or the pleasure of the scene she couldn't tell. Relax, everybody in Angola is always late, she soothed. At least that's what Tiago says, isn't it, that Angolans have no concept of time.

A few minutes later, soaping her body with a sponge, standing in the bath, Ana felt a little more relaxed. This isn't so hard, isn't that difficult after all, she thought. Tiago had already run two pots of water through her hair, his hands surprisingly gentle, but now she was alone again. Remembering Conor and the stories his family had told her about the house in Kimmage, how they'd only had a tin bath for years, taken out every Saturday night. She'd looked in amazement at them, noticing the mixture of pride and amusement on his mother's face. 'Sure they only got the heating five years ago,' Declan, the brother next to Conor had said. 'Not that you'd know,' Conor laughed, 'the oul' fella never puts it on.'

Ana asked herself again if this meeting with Solange could really be happening; wondered what Conor would think of all this, about her having found her mother, or her mother having found her, and finally going to meet her. She wished he were here now so she could tell him, talk to him about how she felt, like she had a few times in the past. Even if mostly she never took the subject of her mother out of its silence, even wondering herself sometimes at her reluctance to share more feelings with him. But too busy, much too busy to give it a lot of thought, silence descending between them again.

One of the things she still missed most about Conor was his family, she thought, the rough and tumble of them pouring in and out of his parents' house, lounging on sofas and taking the piss out of one another. And the simple acceptance they'd always greeted her with, part of the unit as soon as she walked through the door that first time. They'd never been overly gentle or precious with her. Maybe that's why she'd liked them so much, because they'd treated her as though she was one of them, Conor's father asking her about her classes, loaning her an old book on Hollywood, his mother leaning up to kiss her cheek before they went home.

The whoosh of cold water came as a shock when she lifted the bucket and poured it down over her shoulders, wondering how she would appear before her own mother. If she would seem ridiculous, ugly, childish. She let the thought evaporate as she dried herself quickly with a soft towel, then ran the aloe and cucumber body lotion around her breasts, her stomach, manoeuvring her arms so her fingers could reach the whole of her back, before smoothing the remainder into her buttocks, squeezing out more for her legs. These mosquitoes are eating me alive, she noticed as she wrapped the towel back around herself.

Before she opened her make-up bag, took out an orange hairband and pushed the hair out of her face. Looked at herself a long moment again before she began to gently rub the face cream, then the foundation, in. Thinking of those Irish girls who got onto the bus in the morning with one face and left with another. Her index and middle finger lingered on her neck as her eyes took in her own reflection again, before she noticed the time on her mobile and snapped out of it. Reached for her eyeliner and mascara, thinking she still had to do her eyeshadow, her brown eyeshadow. But that she'd leave the lipstick, the red lipstick and the perfume, until last.

Lisbon: December 1969

DARK, DEEP DECEMBER on Rua Silva Carvalho. Up, up the street, pausing outside the glass door of a spacious first-floor apartment, behind the wrought iron of a narrow balcony. Blurred, it all seems blurred at first, but a slow, steady manoeuvre and it comes into focus, the scene on the other side of the glass: the young woman laying the crisp white linen on the long mahogany table, setting down the cutlery. Fifteen, she said fifteen. She holds the knives and forks by their edges and tries not to smudge them with her fingerprints. Heaves the stack of heavy soup bowls in from the kitchen, so formal, so old-fashioned, probably from a dinner service the couple were given for their wedding. There now, time for a cigarette.

She takes one from her pack on the mantelpiece, puts her black cardigan around her shoulders, opens the door and stands out on the balcony. Helena, in a soft black dress, thick black stockings and heels. She strikes a match and lifts it towards her cigarette. Reaches her left hand to the back of her neck and presses her palm gently against her hair, pushing some body into it. She looks down at the street and takes in how damp it is this Christmas Eve, cobblestones so slippery you could slide all the way to the Jardim da Estrela. Her eyes turn to the cafés and shops opposite before they move back down to the street lamps. She shivers and goes back inside, closes the door over but not fully.

It's warmer there but still the tones are muted: various shades and shadows white to grey to black, the furniture soaking up most of the light. 'I put the soup on low. They won't be that long, will they?' she says to José as he comes back into the dining room, lighting a cigarette.

'No, I don't think so,' he answers distractedly, thinking of his parents and his grandparents, his sister, his brother, their children, all of them off at midnight mass. They're only here because Tiago is unwell. Or Helena thinks he is. It's probably nothing, but anyway it got them out of the *Missa do Galo*, a last minute reprieve.

I'll see how he is tomorrow, then take him to the hospital the next day if he's still not well, Helena tells herself. Remembers not to panic because it might be nothing more than a bad cold, brought on by such a sudden drop in temperature. She smiles up at José, skin dark against the black-ribbed polo neck bought yesterday in the Baixa. Nice, to have a morning together again, to drift in and out of the shops, go for a coffee in A Brasileira. Meeting an old friend at Rossio train station, passing him the newspaper with the Brazilian copy of *Luanda* inside, scanning for the PIDE. And then the sharp, still air as they stepped outside again, buying some roasted chestnuts from a smoky cart, Helena looking at the lines of hard years carved into the vendor's face, her missing teeth. Smiling and thanking her, knowing she's glad to be back, but only for a holiday.

Yes, it was somehow so satisfying to be in Lisbon yesterday morning, José thinks, to discover his corners of the city again. Even though all he'd felt on his first evening at home was disappointment after the expectation of the return. Because he *had* been looking forward to coming home, to seeing his family again. Oh, he wasn't ecstatic about the trip, that's true, but there was a certain excitement, a certain giddiness and glamour, in returning for the season. But as his father drove them from the airport all he could think was how small the city seemed. How intimate and real, corners and buildings crowding in on him, taking something from him, telling him who he was, who he would never be.

But then that rush of odd, uncertain joy, at rediscovering his old stomping grounds: the cafés, bookshops, compositions of human forms he'd been a part of, could slip back into so easily. He looks at Helena, noticing how the dress shapes her body.

What more is to be done? she asks herself, picturing the puddings: the *aletria* and the *arroz doce* sitting in the refrigerator, the *rabanadas* and *filhoses* they will fry later. She wonders again if she should put the cod on, but Senhora de Castro said not to worry, to leave it until they had returned from the church. Oh, she's a nice woman, Senhora de Castro, and she was so immediately impressed by Tiago it made Helena feel proud somehow, but she likes things done her way. Helena's surprised she's even been allowed to set the table. Thinks she'll be glad to get to Oporto in a few days, back to her own home, own family. 'Should we light the candles?' she watches José coming towards her.

'Yes, why not,' he replies, but he's no more interested in what she's saying than the beautiful patterns on the tablecloth. He opens his arms wide and shifts into her. Smiles as if he's had a couple of drinks, which he hasn't. Then studies her face warmly and reaches for her mouth with his lips.

His eyes close and he thinks how delicious it would be, his dark sex against the white skin of her thigh. Though there's not enough time. Or maybe, perhaps, if they are quick. His eyes flicker open and he can see Helena is thinking the same thing. So he takes her hand and quickly, quickly leads her to his childhood bedroom.

15

Luanda: January 2007

EYES: ENORMOUS, DARK BROWN, almost black, that was the first thing Ana noticed about her, the younger of the two women sitting at a table shaded by trees. And knew immediately this was her by the clarity of her gaze, how hungrily she seemed to eat her up, like a departed lover somehow miraculously returned. Yes, it was the eyes that gave her away, and that long crooked nose which, Ana recognised now, was so like her own.

'Ana?' she got up in slow motion as Ana felt Tiago drift away, the woman's companion too. Then walked towards her, curled her arms around her body and fell into her breast. '*Aiuê*, my daughter,' Ana heard the wail, and wondered if they might just stay like this all day, flesh to flesh, and let the rest of the world carry on regardless.

Eventually she lifted her head, catching how fixed her mother's stare was as she moved away. 'This is Tiago,' she reached out an open palm, guiding her brother over.

'Tiago...' the woman stood looking at him, Ana watching him squirm slightly, make an attempt to kiss her, then stop halfway. He smiled inanely, unsure of himself. 'A pleasure to see you again, Tiago,' she stepped towards him and he grew confident, kissed her on both cheeks.

'Nice to…' – he seemed to consider something – 'meet you, Solange?' the end of his sentence became a question.

Ana studied the second woman's face as she moved towards her, noticed she was older, definitely older than Solange. 'Ana,' her smile was full of feeling as she kissed Ana, held her briefly, then stood back to take her in, to appraise her head to foot. She shook her head gently, eyes moving up and down. 'I'm Josefa, Solange's sister.'

'This is Tiago,' Ana introduced, and watched as he moved towards the woman, how her eyes took him in. Causing his expression to falter before he cast whatever it was he felt aside and his face became open and warm.

Aunt, yes, that's what Josefa is, isn't she? Ana thought to herself as she turned back to Solange, and saw that her mother was staring at her again, staring at her silently like she wasn't sure she was real, was worried this girl might be an apparition that would vanish without warning.

'Let's have a seat, let's have a drink,' Josefa held out a chair for Ana to sit at the table where two half-empty glasses of beer reminded her they were late.

'Thanks,' she said as she smoothed her dress with the back of her hand. 'I'm so sorry we were late.'

'Don't worry, nothing wrong,' Solange waved the matter away. 'What's a few minutes after all these years. *Senta, senta,*' she motioned Tiago to a chair perpendicular to Ana, sitting herself down opposite her daughter.

'What do you want to drink?' Josefa asked Ana.

'No, let me get it,' Tiago protested. 'What would everybody like to drink?'

'No, no, no,' Josefa wasn't having it. 'I'll go. What do you want, Ana?'

'A beer, please,' she answered, putting her sunglasses back down on her nose. 'And you?' she lifted her chin a little as she addressed Tiago, 'a beer also?'

'Yes, a beer please.' Tiago sat awkwardly down, Ana thinking he probably wanted to get the hell out of here but wouldn't leave her alone just like that. She'd made him swear, after all, to stay until she was ready to go.

'What a charming place,' she said, polite and inconsequential, thinking she and Solange might otherwise just stay looking at one another, leaning slowly into one another, while Tiago was left out of the whole scene.

'I know, I adore it. It's so peaceful, you know, and right in the centre of town. Incredible. Have you been here before, Tiago?'

He nodded his head. 'Yes, my wife Cristina loves it. All the plants,' he gestured towards a woman busy at work in the nursery.

'And there's a shop? What kind of things do they sell?' Ana noticed a small wooden and glass construction.

'They have very sweet things,' Josefa said as she placed the two fresh beers on the table, 'swimsuits, sarongs, things like that. Everything comes from Brazil, no, Solange?'

'Yes,' her sister confirmed, 'from Brazil.'

'Ah, Brazil, I love Brazil,' said Ana. 'Have you been there, Josefa?' she lifted her pack of cigarettes, offered the woman one.

'No, *obrigada*. I don't smoke. I've never been to Brazil, no. Cuba, *sim*. Mexico, *sim*. But Brazil no.' Ana moved the cigarettes toward Solange, watched as her long nails painted a rich cherry removed one from the pack.

'Did you like Cuba?' she tried to keep the conversation going with Josefa as she offered Tiago a cigarette too. Didn't know why she did though, he never smoked her brand, hadn't done so since he was at university and out of money by Monday. He took out one of his own, lit the women's cigarettes, then his.

'Oh, Cuba is marvellous. Another world, another world,' Josefa enthused. 'Life is so simple. And the people, so sweet, so sweet. I'd like to go back, you know. Go back before Fidel dies. God help them when he's gone. Those stupid Americans ready to run in again, take everything over again. Tut, tut, tut, tut,' she picked up a handful of cashew nuts.

'My sister is a communist. You'll have to excuse her. She gets very excited,' Solange smiled at Ana as she exhaled.

'*Sim*, I'm a communist,' Josefa agreed. 'And this place might still be worth something if a few more of us were,' she indicated the world outside the bar with the movement of her arm, about to go off on a rant before she seemed to remember what they were here for and smiled at Ana.

'And do you live here in Luanda now?' Josefa asked Ana, leaving her wondering if Solange had told her anything much at all.

'No, she lives in Ireland,' her sister pointed out, sounding like patience was an essential ingredient in how she conducted her communications with Josefa.

'Ah, Ireland? Yes, that's right. Are they all still against the English there?' Josefa wanted to know.

'Some, but not really that many in the Republic,' Ana had a glimpse of Conor telling his younger sister to get a grip when she began her teenage flirtation with Sinn Féin. 'It's different in the North. But the war is over anyway, nearly ten years now, and the people are trying to get on with life.' Josefa nodded her head very slowly, Ana sure she was thinking something but saying nothing.

She felt distracted again by a presence as she watched Josefa. Turned and, yes, sure enough, there she was again, Solange, looking at her longingly and not even considering turning her eyes away, as if the look was the most casual, natural thing in the world.

'How many are you? How many brothers and sisters do you have?' Ana looked at Josefa, then Solange.

'We're six girls, but no boys,' Solange answered, Ana noticing how luscious the thick curls of her hair were, much shorter and darker than her own.

'Six girls? What?' she blurted out in response, hearing Tiago whistle.

'And are they all living here in Angola?' he asked.

'*Como*?' Josefa said as if she was distracted, a brief, odd look passing over Solange's face.

'I said are they all living here?' he repeated.

'No, no, no,' Josefa shook her head vigorously. 'Carla lives in Paris. Solange was there for more than twenty years as well and then there's…'

'Is that right?' Ana interrupted Josefa's list.

'Yes,' Solange nodded. 'I only came back a few years before the end of the war. But I still spend a lot of time there. It's funny, you know, I'm back here now but my music's starting to really take off over there. I released a CD in France last year. I'll have to give you a copy.' Ana smiled, thinking of the tracks she'd listened to over and over on the computer a few days before, unaware at the time she was actually listening to her mother.

'But tell me, where do the rest of your sisters live, Josefa?' Ana turned back to the other woman.

'Henriqueta is in Cape Town,' Josefa went on.

'Ah yeah?' Ana asked.

'*Sim*,' Josefa nodded. 'Solange and I are here now. Ruth as well, she's the eldest. We had another sister also, next to Solange, but she died. She was called Alice,' her eyes shifted to her younger sister.

'Alice, yes Alice,' Solange murmured in the hush, leaving Ana to try and take everything in.

'And what do you work at in Ireland? You teach film, isn't that it?' Solange put her cigarette out and broke the silence, resting her arms on the table. Allowing Ana to catch a glimpse of her breasts, more ample than her own, so rich against the fresh white linen of her dress with its embroidered blue and green flowers. She listened to a brief thought, quickly smothered, of how this woman was much less whorish than she had at times feared.

'Yes,' Ana confirmed, thinking she was good-looking, yes, but strong, more masculine than she had imagined, her long face handsome rather than pretty really. She admired the chunky wooden bracelet on her left wrist. Thinking she'd made up her mother so often; in pieces, in fragments, it was hard to understand this complete, living, breathing person was the one she had imagined. 'And I'm doing a PhD at the moment,' she went on. She heard a rustling noise and looked over at a bird in the lower branches of one of the trees.

'It's called a *rabo-de-junco*, that bird,' Solange informed her as they listened to the song of the greyish looking bird. 'I love the cinema,' she moved back to what Ana had been talking about. 'There's a beautiful Angolan film, *Nelista*. Have you seen it?' Ana shook her head. 'So you must, it's wonderful. But tell me more about your job.'

'Well, I work in two places,' Ana replied, 'in the National College of Art and Design and University College Dublin. I'm doing my PhD with the art college.'

'And you teach people how to make films?' Solange's face was open, interested.

'No, no, no,' Ana laughed. 'It's more the history of cinema: important movements and periods, things like that. Sometimes more specialised courses as well: fashion in film, the role of space in film.'

She laughed again at the ring of this last title, noticed Josefa taking her in, and wondered whether she was thinking all this was bourgeois rubbish: space, gender, the star system. Sometimes Ana did too, got frustrated with the academics' shoe-horning of the truth into neat theories. And it drove her mad at moments, the fact their writings were often more interested in text than image, so obsessed with meaning they hardly bothered to open their eyes to the visual. As if they forgot that was the whole point of cinema, a series of rapidly moving images flick-tricking the eye. That was why she loved reading film directors themselves talking about cinema: the young *Cahiers du cinéma* critics, Jean Renoir, Satyajit Ray.

'But I would like to make a film in the future,' she let out a nervous giggle. 'Sometimes I film things, you know, and project them for myself after a lecture. Just to see what they look like on a big screen.'

She saw Solange's face projected in an enormous close-up, watched herself touching the image with her hand. Then smiled at Solange, everything seeming to slow down again, wishing once more that they were alone, just the two of them, talking as if they had fooled time, were seated outside it. So that they could give themselves to each other, let the other discover them, slowly unwrap them like a gift. And so she could ask her mother all the questions she'd always wanted.

Luanda: March 1970

THE CLACKING OF A PROJECTOR, flickering image…
of an afternoon: pastel pink walls of the national bank, sky
a duck-egg blue with only a few, few whispers of white
clouds. Down by the Bay of Luanda.

Helena makes her way through the crowd, passing
women wearing masks of pink feathers, children with their
faces painted yellow and orange, young couples kissing.
She scans for a spot where they won't be squashed but will
still have a decent view of the parade. Brushes her hand
along her upper arm, scratches her head. Wondering what
she thinks of her new hairstyle, bob length, thick, full of life
now. She sees some space further along, puts her hands on
the pushchair. 'Let's go,' she smiles down at Tiago.

Idiot, you're such an idiot, José mutters to himself inside
the silence of the apartment. Looking out the window at a
couple of young men in flared jeans, their girlfriends in short
dresses, laughing and making their way down to the parade.
While a heavy woman in a clown's wig strolls slowly along
behind them. He considers opening the window, only the
noise would distract him from his work. And there's still
half a manuscript to read this afternoon. Why did I schedule

the meeting for tomorrow? he asks himself, then wonders for a fleeting moment if there's any chance of changing it, postponing it. Sweet release, relief, the devil of temptation calling him. If he does put the date back he'll be able to go and find Helena and Tiago, to say he's sorry, and then they can enjoy the day together. Then he won't feel so bad.

Faded, colours faded, the afternoon sun so huge in the sky. Helena holds Tiago up and cheers as another troupe passes, dancing in formation, females with bowls of fake fruit on their heads slowly moving their heavy hips, loud whistles on the air. Then a group of *bessangana* women. She encourages Tiago, 'Look, look,' as small boys in gold crowns and cloaks dance up to the spectators, playing up to the captive audience. Why didn't he come? He would have loved it, she remembers José again, alone in the apartment, working his way slowly through the book. And wonders how it can be so complicated, to take an hour away from it and spend their first *carnaval* together. But things are never that straightforward with José. He always leaves everything to the last minute, then tries to do it all perfectly, getting himself into a panic. Another group of children passes, dressed in green, red and yellow, a man carrying a big Portuguese flag. It's so hot. She looks over and up at the sun.

But no, there's no way he can go, take another afternoon off, give over a few hours to enjoying himself. He hasn't got any time. And there's no way he'd dare postpone the meeting with Francisco, who's just starting out, who seems to have come out of nowhere with this novel. No, he wants to do the right thing. Be grown up, responsible. Get on top of things and then maybe he'll have more energy for his own book. Still just an idea and hints of scenes, still only pieces, fragments, but if he had more time he could really get down to it, get working on it.

Guilherme, that's what he'll call his unknowing prophet of Luanda. *Sim*. Guilherme. Or Horácio, what about Horácio? He drifts back over to his white desk, notices how dark the hairs on his arm are against it, and thinks again how things would be better if they had more space, if he had his office back. But they need that other room for Tiago, sleeping on his own a month already, Helena finally giving him up nightly, though still terrified sometimes while she is away from him, in dreams.

The FINA float passes: blue, red, gold and white, glittering, gleaming against the water, picture grainy after all these years. 'Look, Tiago, it's a mermaid,' she points to a green boat with a Queen of the Sea reclining on a seashell in front, waving to the spectators. Then smiles, waves furiously at the woman, and remembers Kianda, mythical mermaid the fishermen are devoted to. The Goddess of the Sea Angolans dance their *semba* to, this *carnaval* itself an offering up to her. She claps again and cheers, wondering what her ex-colleagues would say if they could see her now, behaving like somebody demented.

But let them, let them, the thought forms then flees as striking young women dressed as silver centurions wiggle their almost visible behinds, make light work of the music with their sandalled feet. She moves her shoulders to the beat, looks up at the sun again, its long glinting rays, then back at the whole colourful scene passing in a haze of noise along the Marginal.

16
Luanda: January 2007

THERE WAS SOMETHING SO STRANGE, and yet so entirely natural, about ending up here, Ana was thinking when she heard her mother, yes, her mother, speak. 'Like it?' Solange's eyes were wide, imploring, taking in every tiny movement on Ana's face, sitting across the table from her in the restaurant by São Paolo market. 'Don't like it, no?' Ana swallowed the mouthful of *funge*, looked at the ball of grey gloop sitting on her plate and wondered how she was going to get through all of it. 'It's nothing bad. Lots of people don't like it, it's very Angolan,' Solange went on.

'No, it's not that,' Ana replied. 'It's just unusual, you understand, the texture. We don't have this in Europe. It's just new, different.'

'Okay, okay, but if you don't like it, leave it,' Solange spoke again.

'No, no, no, it's fine,' Ana reassured.

Though in truth she wasn't at all convinced about any of the food before her: the dried fish with its texture like rubber, the unwieldy green leaves, the bowl of beans in palm oil. Even the restaurant had taken her by surprise, how flimsy and half-built it had looked when they walked into its dim interior, out of the dazzling weight of the sun. Though slowly, since they sat down, the place *had* begun to take on a life of its own, to seem real and not merely a poor imitation of a proper restaurant. At least it was better than those corrugated iron eateries outside, with their enormous steaming pots, advertising the drinks they had for sale on wooden tables in front.

'Do you want another beer?' Ana asked Solange.

'*Sim*,' she answered, looking down at her almost empty bottle.

Ana called the waitress over again, after she'd finished writing down an order for another table in a small yellow notepad. 'Two more, please,' she held up her bottle for the woman to carry away, but Solange took it from her hand and placed it back down beside her own.

'No, we keep them here so we know how many beers we've had when it's time to pay,' she insisted. 'No disputes, you know.'

'But they wouldn't rip you off, would they?' Ana thought of Luzia, the heavy woman wearing the black headscarf who ran the restaurant and had come to embrace Solange when she arrived. Who had taken Ana in a bear hug too. '*Esta cabrita, a tua filha?* Your daughter? What a marvel,' she'd said, shaking her head.

Just like the woman with the hardened features in the market, in the green headscarf with pink flowers, who sold alternative medicines, Xica. Another friend of Solange's who'd seemed so delighted to meet Ana. 'She wants to know if you need anything for your man, you know, to keep him going if he's not at his best,' Ana had laughed when Solange told her what the woman had said in Kimbundu. And again when she said that her son would be glad to take her out if she was interested. She thought about the market now, how clean and neat it was, the Indian man selling fabrics at the back, and what Solange had told her about Xica. How she'd walked all the way from Malanje with her baby on her back during the war.

'Eh, don't you believe it!' Solange brought Ana's mind back to the beer bottles. 'Everybody here is out to make whatever money they can.' Ana smiled, looked around the restaurant, and thought again about the meeting the day before, about how she still couldn't really take it all in, finding Solange. And Josefa. Stubborn, funny Josefa. She remembered her saying she only had one son when they spoke about children. And then Solange herself saying she didn't have any, except for Ana, that she was the only one.

'What's Josefa doing today?' Ana wondered.

'I'm not sure. I think she said she has some kind of a meeting with OMA, the *Organização da Mulher Angolana*. Have you heard of it?'

'Yes, of course,' Ana thought about the demonstration she'd passed in the car with Cristina, the hundreds of women with yellow headscarves, how her sister-in-law had honked the horn in support.

'She's very political, my sister,' Solange shook her head. 'Too much sometimes. Have to tell her to leave it out, that you don't need to be indoctrinated. Ruth is even worse. *Aka!* Wait until you meet her. That's all she wants to talk about. Now don't say I didn't warn you!' she lifted her finger and laughed.

Then paused for a moment before she began speaking again, quickly, as if she didn't want any silence to form between them. 'I remember when we got our first radio, what a novelty it was,' she began, 'and all I wanted to do was to dance and sing along to the Congolese music, the Brazilian and Cuban music, you know. I was mad for music, especially then, being a teenager.' She shook her head. 'But for them, for Ruth and Josefa, my father as well, it was like a political tool, the radio. What they were interested in were the broadcasts from the rebels.'

'From the MPLA?' Ana asked.

'*Sim*, my family was always with the MPLA,' Solange continued, 'And there was a programme every evening, seven o'clock on the dot, *Angola Combatente*. My sisters never missed that. Oh, I listened to it as well sometimes, eh, but they were obsessed with it. Crouching under the kitchen table, the transistor on just low enough to make out what the voices were saying. You didn't want to be found listening to the programme.'

'But was it really so dangerous here at the time?' Ana looked intently at Solange.

'It was, it was, child. Those Portuguese, don't get me started. The things they did, Ana. And the PIDE were much worse here than in Portugal, you know. If they thought you were working for independence, a "terrorist" they called it, you had no hope.' She whistled. 'They were brutal, really brutal. We lost an uncle to them. Tortured to death because he wouldn't give them the information they wanted.' She looked away, then back at Ana. '*Angola Combatente* was absolutely forbidden. Not that people didn't listen, eh. So many people did, families like us; some in the bath, some with pillows over their heads. Girls saying they were going to *bençon*, you know this special mass they have at seven in May, when they were really going home to listen to the show. Your father as well.' There was a pause as Ana watched a number of flies moving across the plastic tablecloth, wondered if she should say something about him, about José, open up their story, his history with Solange, but she looked away instead and let the moment drift. Thinking she just wanted to let her mother take her with her, wherever she was going, leaving the complications, the recriminations, for another day.

She could feel Solange watching her carefully, heard her break the silence again after a moment and looked up. 'I remember when that first radio was stolen,' she let out another low whistle, leaving Ana to study the soft skin of her face beneath the lilac scarf wound around her hair, eyes moving down to her black vest, dressed more casually today. 'Most people were just starting to get radios back then, you know,' she continued. 'It wasn't like now with these iPods and all that. Was a big deal. Some of the richer families in Bairro Indígena had them but we didn't get one until 1967, '68, and when we got it, it was never turned off. But then one morning we woke up early to find it was gone, just gone!'

'Somebody had stolen the radio?' Ana egged the other woman on, wanting her to make the story a good one.

'*Sim*, senhora,' Solange's voice seemed to grow self-consciously grave. 'It was only a transistor radio, you know. Small, cream, one of those Bakelite ones, but we loved it. Had it on from early in the morning right until my mother went to bed well after midnight. She'd always stay up late, you know, cleaning the apartment. Singing along to American jazz tunes even though she couldn't speak a word of English. Ella Fitzgerald, Dinah Washington, Billie Holiday.'

'I adore Billie Holiday,' Ana felt herself become immersed in the scene.

'She was the Queen, it's true,' Solange agreed. 'Until today I love Billie. My father had a few of her records, you know, on vinyl, and I used to listen to them on his old gramophone player. It was ancient, Ana,' she shook her head slowly. 'Had belonged to my grandfather, the Portuguese one, come all the way from Lisbon. So old, so heavy,' Solange slapped her leg. 'We thought it was a dinosaur, but Billie sounded just great coming out of it; the sound of the record turning, the crack in her voice. Aye, Ana, always I connect Billie with that old gramophone.'

Something caught Ana's eye then: a good-looking young man in a smart white shirt walking across the dust floor of the restaurant, sitting down at a table. She supposed he must be on his lunch break, chanced another forkful of fish and returned her gaze to Solange. 'And the radio, what happened about the radio?' she pressed, eyes brightening in anticipation.

'Ah, the radio. Yeah, they were going missing a lot around then, you know. Suddenly loads of people had them but still there were others who couldn't afford them. Didn't stop them though. Many, many radios were stolen during that time. You have to tie some things down in this country if you want to keep them, you know. And it's much, much worse nowadays. Tut, tut!' Solange shook her head in irritation, in resignation, then looked Ana straight in the eye again. 'When Josefa saw it was gone, there was war. Phew! She knew exactly who it was and went running out the door to get him. All of us followed behind, of course.'

'I wouldn't fancy messing with Josefa,' Ana laughed. 'What did she do?'

'Oh, she went straight to the boy's mother. It was a boy who lived on the same street, you know. The mother used to take in washing from the *tugas*, the Portuguese, and she was already up washing the sheets or whatever. So Josefa said to her that her son had taken their radio, that he'd already taken a couple from a few people around the neighbourhood, had been seen selling them down at the market. She demanded the radio back.'

'And what did she say, the woman?' Ana wanted to know.

'*Olha*, Senhora Gonçalves was one of these women whose kids could do no wrong, you know this type?' Ana nodded. 'A good woman, don't get me wrong. Worked hard, did everything for those kids, that layabout of a husband, but they were lazy bastards, the lot of them. And Daniel was a little runt, a little runt with a big mouth. Would have been around sixteen, same age as Josefa at the time. And his mother knew what he was like, what he used to get up to, but nobody could say anything against her kids, especially Daniel.

'But you know what Josefa is like, Ana. You saw her yesterday. Once she gets something into her head, that's the end of it. Keeps on and on at it like a little dog. Oh, Senhora Gonçalves denied it all right, started making a big fuss, shouting, saying Daniel would never do anything like that, he was a good boy, and who was this girl to walk in here accusing her son of something he'd never done. But Josefa wasn't intimidated, wasn't frightened of her. She listened for a few moments, then turned and walked straight into the woman's home with her following behind, screaming. She didn't care though, just went right into the room where the boy was sleeping and grabbed him by the scruff of the neck. Asked him where the radio was and when he said he knew nothing about it she said she would give him to the count of ten to tell her. "*Um, dois, três...*" she counted but he still wouldn't answer.' Solange shook her head, barely repressing a grin.

'So then she dragged him down to where his mother

had been washing the clothes. Just in his knickers and vest,' she chortled now. 'Pulled him over to the water and held his head above it. Said if he didn't tell her she'd dunk him. He was almost crying but still he wouldn't tell her. And the mother was hysterical, screaming, all the other kids out on the balcony, laughing at Daniel squirming. "One more chance. I'll give you one more chance," she promised but when he still didn't answer she put his head straight into the water, suds and all, held it under. Only ten seconds, it wasn't long, but he came up wailing, crying like a baby. Told her the radio was under his bed. Said he was sorry, so sorry. But Josefa just said if he tried anything like that on her or any of her family again, he wouldn't be so lucky. He was still crying in his mother's arms when we left the place,' Solange's laughter echoed through the restaurant, Ana laughing along with her mother now too.

Luanda: August 1970

Day 1

HELENA, STANDING IN THE KITCHEN of the new apartment, turns on the gas, strikes a match and sees the blue flame shoot to life. Puts the cream-coloured kettle back on the burner, half-full. Moves the stainless-steel plunger along the worktop, takes the yellow coffee container in her hand and lifts the top off. Opens the drawer where the cutlery is kept and lifts a teaspoon with a pale blue handle out. Lays it down next to the coffee container. Rests her hand on the counter. Presses her lips together and stares vacantly at the sink. She notices a mark on the white tiles with the orange and brown flower patterns. Takes the sponge in her hand and wipes them. Puts some detergent on the sponge, rinses it under the water and lays it in its dish beside the sink. Then removes her wedding ring, places it on the counter, squirts some detergent into her palm and rinses her hands. Dries them slowly, meditatively, on the tea towel.

She takes a look at the kettle again but it still isn't boiling. Remembers that she hasn't chosen a cup yet, then takes one from the shelf above the table. Finds its saucer and puts them together on the counter. Walks from the kitchen into the bright white sitting room to see if Tiago is okay in his playpen. He is, so she smiles, then walks back to the kitchen, hand smoothing her yellow and white gingham housecoat as she goes. The kettle is whistling. She watches the steam rising, runs her fingers between her hair and neck. Thinks that she has to buy some new shoes for Tiago. That he's growing so quickly. She'll get them on Saturday morning. She turns the kettle off. Lifts it over to the counter top, scalds the plunger, puts the kettle down, puts three spoons of coffee into it. Lifts the kettle and fills the steel apparatus almost to the top. Puts the lid on and returns the kettle to the cooker. Waits while the coffee brews.

Day 2

THE MARKET IS LOUD and full of movement when Helena walks in wearing navy flared trousers, a fitted denim shirt, a brown cardigan, with Tiago in his pushchair. Most days she comes here to get what she needs for lunch, dinner, breakfast. Could ask Margarida, the girl who comes in an hour a day to do the shopping, but she prefers doing it herself. Arriving at eight in the morning usually, when the set-up is well over but the food is still fresh.

'Good morning, senhora!' the seller Helena always goes to says in a thick Portuguese accent. 'How can I help you today?'

'I would like half a kilo of bananas,' Helena begins. The woman holds them up for inspection and she nods her approval before they are lifted over to the scales.

'Anything more?' she asks.

'A kilo of oranges,' Helena replies, then watches the hard-working hands reach out over the tiers of colours.

Notices how short the nails are.

'Anything more?' she asks again.

'How are the mangoes today?'

'Rich, good and sweet,' the market trader lifts one up, Helena inspecting the pink blush of it.

'Give me half a kilo then,' she says.

'Anything more?'

Helena doesn't answer.

'*Ó* senhora, anything more?'

'Half a kilo of potatoes and a big head of broccoli,' Helena snaps out of it.

'Anything more?' the woman asks a few moments later but Helena shakes her head, then pays. Walks over to the fish seller from Lobito in the cream headscarf and asks her for two good-sized *postas* of salmon. Because it's salmon, isn't it, she'd planned to cook for lunch today?

Day 3

SEVEN O'CLOCK. José will be home again in half an hour. Time to begin the meal. Helena goes into the sitting room, takes Tiago in her arms, puts him in his high chair in the kitchen. Does this every day when she's cooking dinner, talking or singing to him as she prepares the meal. She goes to the small room where she stores the vegetables, breaks off a few cloves of purple-coloured garlic and takes a good quantity of spinach. What was the other thing I needed for this dish? she jogs her memory as she walks towards the counter top, looking at the orange and brown flowers on the tiles again. Olives, she opens the fridge, takes them and two big beef tomatoes out. The codfish as well, wrapped in its greaseproof paper. She lifts the frying pan down off the wall. Lights the gas, extinguishes the match, puts the pan on top and pours in a layer of olive oil.

The chopping board, that's what she needs to cut the garlic into small pieces. She crouches down and opens the cupboard but it's not there. Not there? she scratches her temple lightly, then stands up and looks around, is relieved to see it on the draining board. Why didn't I dry it earlier? she asks herself, can't understand the omission. She always dries the dishes as soon as she's washed them, hates them clogging up the area, making the kitchen look so messy. She slides a knife from its set, the small one she uses for cutting garlic. Cuts the bottom of the first clove off, just a sliver from the end, then peels the skin away and starts to slice slowly into it.

And when all the tiny pieces of garlic are together in a small pile she drops them into the pan. Noticing Tiago is looking at her as she turns to wash the spinach, wondering what he's thinking. Only realising a few moments later that the garlic is burning in the pan. She tuts loudly, turns the gas down and moves the pan to another ring.

17

Luanda: January 2007

ANA TOOK ANOTHER SIP OF HER COFFEE in the Lebanese café where she and Solange had come after lunch, her mind turning to an image of the woman as a tall teenage girl, thirty-five years before. 'It was an uncle,' her mother was saying, an uncle who played percussion with the band. 'It was with him I first started singing for an audience, down at the Liga Africana, sometimes in the cinemas for the Portuguese.' She went on to tell Ana about the couple of times she'd been on television, while Ana took in her sumptuous brown mouth, felt captivated by the upbeat, talkative figure who stood out so against the white walls of the new café.

'I was just a backing singer really,' Solange was still talking about the TV appearances. 'Another girl and I, both in *panos*. Hard to believe that was me; so young, so innocent. Tut, tut!' She shook her head and closed her eyes for a moment. Leaving Ana to take another nibble of her *pastel de nata*, trying to imagine what it must have been like for Solange, what music had meant to her. She noticed how many waiters and waitresses there were in the place, some wiping tables, some just inventing tasks to complete.

'And did you always sing, even before you first

performed in public?' she asked.

'Oh yes!' 'Solange was emphatic. 'Sing, I think I must have come out of the womb singing. I sang all the time. We used to go to parties, you know, from when I was a kid. Every Saturday afternoon, in the houses of my uncles, aunts. In the *quintais*, the backyards in the *musseques*. Lots of food, all my cousins. And always there was music. My uncle Rodrigo would start to play the guitar. And we'd go on like that for hours. I adored singing, eh. Dancing and singing with my cousins from when I was this high,' she lowered her hand to two feet above the ground.

And as Ana saw the movement she pictured her mother for a moment as a very young girl. Thought slowly of the three children at the end of *Orfeu Negro*, sitting at the edge of a cliff overlooking the Bay of Rio, the boy playing the guitar causing the sun to rise with his music. The light, the light changing to yellow, brightening their tiny faces.

'*Toma essa florzinha*.' Ana smiled again, seeing the girl in the white dress offering a flower to the guitar-playing boy. '*Toca uma musiquinha para mim. Toca*,' she could hear the sweet Brazilian voice asking him to play her a little song. '*Oh la la la, Oh la la la*,' the three of them skipping along and dancing now, the sky a cloudless blue. '*Oh la la la, la la la la la la la la…* '

'I remember my grandmother asking me when I was about eight what I wanted to be,' Ana tuned back into what Solange was saying. 'And knowing I wanted to be a singer but too shy to say it, you know. I didn't answer, just stood there like a fool while she looked down at me. Telling me I'd become a secretary, a civil servant, like the older girls in the family, my sisters. And I can still remember thinking, You're wrong, Granny, I'm not like them, I'm different. I'm going

to be a singer. Yeah, I knew even then what I wanted to do.'
Ana thought it was true, how she could only picture Solange
as a strong-willed child.

'I was so determined, you know. And that's why I was
so happy to sing with my uncle's band,' Solange continued.
'But I was shy. You wouldn't believe it now, but I was so shy.
Afraid of my own shadow, intimidated by everything. *Olha*,
I knew it was what I wanted to do, but I was still so petri-
fied. I shook like a leaf that first night.'

Ana could envisage her getting ready with the other girl.
'And your family? Were they there for those first concerts?'
she asked Solange.

'Oh, my father was,' she replied. 'He would only let me
sing if he walked with me to the venue and then walked
me home. He didn't drink, you know. He was very old-
fashioned. Very straight-laced.' My grandfather, that would
make him my grandfather, Ana thought as if in response.
'Very upright, you know. But he adored the music. *Adored*
it,' Solange's intonation became more pronounced. 'The
accordion, the accordion was his instrument. And he knew
I was wild about music too; always dancing, always singing.
Maybe he thought if it was he who set things up, if he was
my chaperone, then everything would be fine, I'd be satis-
fied,' Solange said.

'Because prostitutes worked in some of the clubs, you
know,' she went on, 'and the singers had to be careful, some
people didn't know the difference between the two. And
there were, yes, there were a few singers who were bad,
went with lots of men. I'm not saying anything but... you
know.'

She looked at Ana, down at her coffee cup. 'Finished?'
'Yes,' Ana confirmed.

'Okay, come on, there's a shop I want to show you near here. It has lovely stuff,' Solange took her arm as they walked to the door, bringing Ana right back to the present.

Luanda: February 1971

HERE THEY ARE AGAIN, José and Helena. Early Friday afternoon, on the road to Mussulo, the other way of getting to the 'island'. José is at the wheel of the baby-blue convertible, its top down, his aftershave lingering on the breeze. Wearing tortoiseshell sunglasses, a freshly pressed white shirt, tapered tan-coloured slacks and light brown moccasins. Flares? No, no, no. It might be 1971 but José likes the way clothes were made a decade before. He has a tailor here, a tiny old *mulato* from Lubango who he goes to a couple of times a year. Can't, can't abide this cheap rubbish coming in: denim and polyester that hugs the crotch and is wide enough at the ends to sweep the streets. Though his hair is a little longer; he has made some concession to the changing times.

Helena turns the dial of the radio. Static, fado, Ngola Ritmos, the Rolling Stones. She settles for the last of these, leans back in her seat and shakes her head. Looks up at the sun and lets the nights and days to come wash over her. The time they'll spend at a friend's house, lying in the sun, swimming, cooking the fish they catch on the fire outside, in the shade of a huge old tree. She feels a gentle tremble along her thigh, like a spider crawling beneath the red and white polka dot dress she's wearing. Manoeuvres her feet out along the beechwood of her navy Scholl sandals, running her toes over the buckles at the front, again and again.

José turns from the wheel, looking right behind him. 'Our first weekend away together in a year and a half,' he says out loud and winks.

'Who are you speaking to?' Helena wants to know.

'To the audience, of course,' he replies.

'Oh yes,' she looks around too and smiles. Before they turn back towards the road and she puts her arm around him, rests her head on his shoulder. Both looking out the windscreen now as they drive past palm trees, coconut trees, sand and the shimmer of the ocean.

But maybe that never happened, José and Helena heading off to Mussulo for the weekend, a Friday evening in February 1971. Maybe he's in the car, yes. And it's a baby-blue convertible, okay. And the top is down, sure. And he's still heading for thirty but not looking too bad on it, right? But the music blaring from the radio could be a violent rumba beat with Kimbundu lyrics screeching out, not the Stones. Even if it's still a Friday, after work, the sun not going anywhere fast.

And perhaps he's whistling along to the music as he drives, José, thinking of how his manhood strained for her under his desk, in the bathroom. For his Rosa or Anita, young but already so good at being bad. Girls, girls, so many pretty girls. With milk-chocolate skin or breasts as dark as crude oil. Teeth white and sharp like tigers, nipples hard, enormous. Oh, the beauty of their open bodies. The sea revealing its sandbanks to his right.

And yet that might not be it either. Perhaps it didn't all

begin then, only much later. His dalliances, his dreams. It's very possible he *doesn't* go off to be with a younger love early on a Friday evening.

That he doesn't even have the car with him. And instead has just one beer with his uncle Vicente after work, with the other men and women from the office, before heading home. Walking the streets to the apartment where they've lived for more than six months already, listening to the workers sighing after their week and the young people (that was him too, not so long ago) gearing up for the weekend.

And who's to say, this might be one of those nights he isn't blaming himself for being a bad husband, for emotions deferred, trips put off, loaded glances at beautiful asses you could linger in forever. He might arrive home ten minutes later, wondering if there's anything on TV tonight, if there is a play on the radio. Realise he's still in time for this evening's *Angola Combatente*. Though he'll have to be careful, the neighbour came to the door last night while he was listening to it. Had to move quickly to the bathroom.

Yes, perhaps that's it. Yes. He gets home and she's in the kitchen, Helena. Apartment silent, Tiago in bed. And the light catches her hair, the pale skin of her neck, makes her look fragile, beautiful as she stands by the window. He walks gently towards her, kisses her on the neck. Takes her hand and guides her to the bedroom where he will undress her, and she him. Slowly, slowly.

And afterwards she holds him. Holds him and forgives him, for what he is not, cannot be.

18

Luanda: January 2007

THE LOUD HONK OF A HORN. Ana was lifted from her daydream, framed by the plate-glass window of the café, wearing her cream dress with the small orange flowers down its front, her Peggy Cummins in *Gun Crazy* sunglasses. She looked up, saw the small red car with Solange inside, and waved at her. Stubbed her cigarette out with the toe of her shoe and walked towards her. '*Bom dia,*' she kissed the fragrant skin of the woman's cheeks as she slid into the car, taking in the orange cloth wound around her head. 'I bought this for you,' Ana handed her a small paper bag.

'Oh nice, I love chocolate croissants, but you shouldn't have!'

Ana smiled, looked down, then back at her. 'Would you like a coffee? Can I get you a take-away coffee or anything?'

Solange waved her away with her hand. 'No, no thanks, dear. I've had too much already today.'

Ten minutes later they were moving slowly along one of the city's dusty avenues, heading to a friend of Solange's to drop something off, before they went for lunch on the Ilha. 'What are they doing?' Ana asked when the car had stalled, pointing a finger at a long line of women, most of them dressed in traditional fabrics.

'Going in to have their babies,' Solange answered. 'It's a maternity hospital.'

'*Sim*?' Ana squinted, moved closer to the window, making out a number of swollen bellies.

'Yeah. And you know you have to pay for a bed here,' Solange went on. 'Bribe the midwife too. Otherwise you're just left there. Forget about it.' Ana looked back at her. 'Own oxygen, everything. You see women going in with their cans of it. Needles and thread also, to get sewn up afterwards.'

'Are you serious?' Ana was shocked.

'Serious?' Solange's eyes met hers straight on. 'I wish I wasn't. It's a shame, a disgrace. Can you imagine queuing for hours like that?'

'But it must be so dangerous. How can they survive that?' Ana wanted to know.

'They don't... always,' said Solange. 'Some of the babies die. The mothers as well, eh. Infections, complications. But if you don't pay up nobody's going to help you. Might get unlucky and that's it,' she shook her shoulders. 'Many women have their babies in the car park, you know.'

'And me, was I born there?' Ana seized the moment after a brief silence. Had promised herself she wouldn't let such questions simply drift away again, not today.

'Oh no, no, no. I went to Lubango to have you,' Solange answered. 'Stayed with a friend of Josefa's. Went there when I was six months gone. I managed to hide you pretty well until then,' she smiled at Ana. 'But I had to be very careful, you know. In case I met anybody who knew the family in Lubango. I was so frightened my father would find out, you know. He'd always stood up for me, had allowed me to go and study at the music school, even though my mother was against it. And there I was, twenty years old and pregnant by a married Portuguese man. I felt so alone, you know, so frightened and lost. Completely lost.'

Ana looked out at the road again, thinking of Leslie Caron climbing the stairs to her L-shaped room. 'And what was it like, the birth?' she turned back to Solange.

'Oh, it was agony,' Solange shook her head. 'And I'm sure I made it worse because I was so frightened. Josefa was supposed to come to Lubango, but it was chaos trying to get across the county at the time, everybody moving around, all of the Portuguese leaving. And then I went early. Was in the supermarket one morning when my waters broke. And I felt so ashamed, so silly. I didn't know what to do, didn't want to draw any more attention to myself. Just walk, walk to the hospital, I told myself. It isn't far away. And somehow I managed to get there on my own, somehow I managed to get seen, even though many of the doctors were leaving the country by that time.'

'Incredible,' Ana studied Solange's face, the other woman's eyes on the road. 'And was it long, the labour?'

'No, not in the end,' Solange turned to her and smiled again. 'Three, maybe four hours. Some of them were in labour for more than a day. I pitied those women, really pitied them. I mean the pain was terrible, appalling, but it didn't go on that long for me in the end.' Solange inched the car forward. 'And when you came out I couldn't believe it was you. I felt this heat, this intense heat on my chest, and when I looked down there you were. They'd laid you on top of me. *A minha filha*, my own true daughter,' Solange beamed. 'And you were beautiful, perfect, with your tiny fingernails, your full head of hair. I couldn't believe that I'd made you.'

She looked at Ana then, looked her straight in the eye, in silence, Ana still too surprised by everything to react. Stranded without words and thinking about that baby lying on Solange's chest. Experiencing the strange sensation that that was her, was Ana. Wondering now who she might have been if they had stayed together, had stuck together.

Luanda: December 1972

A PHOTOGRAPH OF A DINNER DANCE, New Year's Eve 1972, Cine Tropical, Luanda. Photographer unknown. Two couples smiling, bright saturated colours. The men are wearing tuxedos, José and the other fellow with the slimmed-down beard and big glasses. Yes, that must be Ricardo, one of his colleagues from the publisher's, who translates documents for the MPLA sometimes. After work, after hours. And his wife, what was her name? Ah, Laura, yes, in a cream gown that reaches almost to the floor, an orange sash around her waist, a small cape that goes with the outfit resting on her narrow shoulders. Her husband has his arm around her and her own free hand is curled around the black fabric of Helena's dress. Almost floor-length also, with its sparkling white piping. Complemented by a soft white scarf as long as the dress, and white gloves.

The next snap looks almost the same but now they've swapped places and Ricardo has his arm around Helena, while she is holding Laura's waist and José is resting his hand on his colleague's wife's shoulder. Smiling, still smiling.

Then another one, José guiding Helena to the beat of the

band playing on stage, both surprised, taken off guard, by the flash of the photographer's bulb.

But Laura and Ricardo are much more relaxed in their shot, or Laura at least, because she knew what was coming, could sense the photographer there. Almost a pose from a fashion magazine as they glide across the polished hard-wood floor.

Then an image of the dinner, the four of them around an ornate seafood arrangement, deciding who will begin.

And a moment later José holding a lobster in his hand, a look of horror on his face, as if the crustacean is about to attack him.

With Laura holding her plate up to the camera in the next one, the orange pink of the prawns against the white ceramic.

Before a shot of Helena and Ricardo laughing, laughing at something one or other of them has said.

With another picture from later on in the night, of the couples dancing once more, having swapped partners again. Caught in a split second of a *semba* beat.

Which must come before the moment where they're toasting the New Year with glasses of champagne, just past the stroke of midnight (can see the hour in the big clock behind them.) Next to the cheap gold of the banner, *Próspero Ano Novo!* Happy New Year! Streamers are falling through the air, a paper whistle is blown halfway to its full length by Laura and José, and Ricardo's eyes are shining with alcohol.

But wait, there's one they didn't know about, one José and Helena weren't aware of at the time. A quiet, quiet shot. Where they're holding hands, the couple, her back half to the camera, his jacket off, dickie-bow discarded.

Before finally the last snap, of the foursome leaving

the building. In the *madrugada*. The women with the men's black jackets around their shoulders, hair slightly dishevelled, and their companions still laughing, all four of them stepping out into the future.

19

Luanda: January 2007

'*SUKUA!*' ANA LISTENED TO THE WORD again, sitting beside Solange in her car, after their lunch on the Ilha. Wondering exactly what it meant as she realised, slowly, they were stranded among a multitude of cars. 'Shouldn't have come down this way, tut,' Solange looked around to see if she could manoeuvre herself out, head off down a side street. But she was blocked on all sides. 'This street gets really bad sometimes. It's worse when it rains,' she explained.

'But why, why are there so many cars here?' Ana wanted to know, thinking Luanda was even worse than Dublin, where everybody had a new motor or was busy upgrading. She saw herself sitting on the bus to UCD, progress stalled by the long lines of snaking, shining metal.

'Everybody wants a car in Luanda,' Solange answered. 'Some guys even sleep in their cars, eh. Don't have anywhere to live, have put all their money into a fancy new set of wheels, thinking it's going to get them somewhere, but they end up living out of it.' She shook her head. 'I went to an awards ceremony last year,' she laughed, 'and one of the winners started shaking his car keys from the stage, showing everybody he'd just bought a big new jeep.'

Ana laughed too, 'Are you serious?'

'I am,' said Solange, shaking her head, leaving Ana to visualise a heavy man in a white suit grinning broadly. 'Everybody just wants to get rich here, make a packet,' Solange continued as Ana caught sight of a girl in jeans and a red top walking the dusty sidewalk. 'That's why you have so many people trying to get into politics now, you know. It's where the money is.' She moved the car forward slightly. 'Kids all wanted to be singers when I was younger: the fame, the money, the girls, you know. But now they see the politicians with their sweet houses, their brand new cars and they want what they've got.'

Ana looked back at Solange. 'I suppose it was different before, back when the country was Marxist, no?' she wondered aloud.

'Marxist? Don't make me laugh,' Solange retorted, Ana suddenly remembering what Luísa had said about Zicko Povão, the singer Solange and her cousin had worked with: 'He's dead, Ana. Killed by the government on the twenty-seventh of May.' She felt the car move slightly forward again but knew they weren't going anywhere fast.

'You were in trouble, in trouble with the government before, weren't you?' she turned to Solange.

The other woman looked at her, eyes wide. 'Who told you? Who told you that? Was it Tiago?'

'No, no, no, it wasn't Tiago. I went to see this woman. A singer, Luísa. When I was trying to find you. She said a musician you used to work with back then had been killed by the government,' Ana looked around, lowered her tone, seeing Solange's hands tensing on the wheel.

'Luísa. Of course, Luísa,' she said. 'What more did she tell you?'

'Nothing really,' Ana replied. 'Just that you and your cousin used to sing with him and he'd been killed in some kind of a coup.'

Solange looked back out towards the road. 'Factionalism, that's what it was. Factionalism,' her voice was almost a whisper, Ana's breathing turning shallow beside her. 'You know everything was a mess here after April '74 and the Carnation Revolution?' Ana nodded. 'The time of the Portuguese was over here and everybody wanted to take control: the MPLA, the FNLA, UNITA.' Ana watched as she lifted her fingers, smoothed out one eyebrow, then the other. 'And a lot of people in the *musseques* here in Luanda came out in support of the MPLA, you know. Organised themselves, fought off the FNLA. And the whites as well, when they started trouble, began attacking Africans because they were going to lose everything.' She kept her eyes on the road.

'It was chaos, a crazy time, Ana,' her voice remained low as the car began moving again. 'The Cubans on our side, the Congolese trying to get in, the South Africans sticking their noses in. But you know what happened, the MPLA got rid of the FNLA, took over in November '75. Not very long after I had you,' she caught Ana's eye for a moment before putting her foot on the brake as they came to another halt.

'Anyway, after the MPLA were in power, some of the people and some of these organisations from the *musseques* that had emerged in the fight decided they didn't want anybody telling them what to do. Some of the unions were the same, you know. They'd taken up arms, risked their lives for the good of the common people and now they had the new party elite bossing them round. They'd had a dream. A dream of a new Angola under Agostinho Neto, but things hadn't worked out exactly like that.'

The car began to move slowly again. 'And they, we, the people who didn't like the way the government was running the country still thought we could create some kind of revolution, a utopia,' she continued. 'A free and equal Angola.'

'Didn't Zicko support the government in the beginning though? Luísa told me he travelled around the country with some kind of a delegation after independence?' Ana asked.

'Oh, he did, he did,' Solange nodded confirmation. 'He was a big supporter of the government at the start, Zicko. Sang at their rallies, their dinners, the big events they had. Me too. My cousin Eunice as well, the one in your photo. Zicko was so hopeful, so hopeful to start with,' Solange braked again.

'But he was one of the musicians known for criticising the leadership, you know. Said exactly what was wrong with the new government.'

'And they didn't like that?' Ana was calm, alert, wanted to let her mother know she was listening, was there beside her.

'No, they didn't like it at all,' Solange's voice seemed emptied out as the car moved on again. 'I was there when they took him, you know? Was living with him in Sambizanga at the time, or staying with him most nights anyway, in 1977. He'd always liked me, Zicko, and I'd always pushed him away, but something was starting between us then. Something… I don't know. Anyway, there'd been rumours for days about a coup. Everybody whispering that Nito Alves and Zé Van Dunem were going to take over, going to give real power back to the people. And then we woke up on the 27th of May to shots being fired. Heard a kid shouting outside that the Nilistas had taken over the radio station, the prison. And Zicko was up, putting on his clothes, all fired up and ready to go when they came in. Bam, they just broke down the door and dragged him away. Gave me a few slaps as well when I tried to stop them.'

Ana watched the shadows on her mother's face. 'It was the last time I saw him, last time anybody did. And they didn't even have the decency to give his family a death certificate. Body found by the side of the road with a load of others. *Aiuê*, daughter, he was only twenty-five. Only twenty-five years on this earth.'

Ana reached out her hand to her mother's arm, faltered for a moment, then let her fingers caress her skin. 'Is that why you went to live in France?' she asked softly.

Solange turned her gaze away from the grey waters of the bay, '*Sim*, yes, it was then I left. If you were associated with the coup you had no chance, you know. I was lucky, I suppose. Others disappeared, went missing. I was so afraid they'd come back for me, that they'd take me. And my sister Carla was living in France, so I thought maybe I'd just go and sit things out for a while, wait until things died down back home. Tut! In the end I stayed over twenty years. Strange, isn't it? It was so unusual, so different when I first arrived, but I got used to it, over time.'

'And that was why you changed your name, was it?' Ana asked another question. 'Because of Zicko?'

'I suppose so,' Solange answered, seeming tired now, 'but that was much later on, you know. And I never changed my name officially, it's only for singing.' Ana kept her gaze steady. 'I suppose I didn't want any associations with those times, those terrible times, you know. And I didn't want to attract any enemies.' She let out a sigh. 'Here, let's go this way,' she spotted a way to exit the traffic jam and swung the car to the right while horns blared all around them.

Luanda: May 1973

A SATURDAY MORNING. Helena, sitting in her salmon-coloured slip, looks again at her own reflection. Opens the jar of Nivea and places several spots of cream on her face, her neck. She breathes deeply, then pauses. 'But wouldn't it be better for him to start school there, in Portugal?' she continues talking to the blurred image behind her. 'I mean, we're going to return, sooner or later. Don't you think it's time to face it? We can't stay here forever.' She begins to smooth the cream into her skin.

Then tunes out of her own image after a moment and into the reflection of the bedroom: the yellow blanket on the bed, orange reading lamp on the white ledge behind it, amber-coloured glass of water. With José, still in his green pyjamas, but with a moustache, a thick moustache now, reading the morning papers. And he, he wants to shout out loud, because he's fed up of all this talk about leaving, about returning to Portugal. Petty, pining Portugal. He won't go back, he won't. He slips a hand beneath the right lens of his glasses, wipes his eye. 'But the schools are good here too. And Tiago's already enrolled. Why do you want to go and change everything now?' he asks.

'Not all of the teachers are good,' Helena focuses on her own face again. 'Look, it's not that I can't wait to go back to Lisbon or Oporto. Maybe, I don't know, maybe I'd stay here if we could, but there's no future here. You know it's ending, you know it's nearly all over. Look at Zaïre, at Nigeria, independent more than ten years. They've all gone: the Belgians, the English, the lot of them. We're only hanging on, just hanging on here.' She looks past herself and out at José, to see if he is listening, if anything she is actually saying is registering on his face. But he only seems to want the conversation to be over so he can get back to his papers, his books, that novel he still hopes to write... twenty pages into it, years later. When, exactly when, did he stop listening to me? she wonders.

And it's true, he won't think about, won't consider, not really, what Helena is saying. He has no intention of moving to Lisbon. Why would he? So that Tiago can grow up like he did? No, no, no. But he can sense Helena's scrutiny, doesn't know what to say. 'Anyway, the Portuguese aren't going to leave any time soon. It's not as though they're losing the war,' he stumbles in protest. Then chides himself, thinking, why did I say that? Why on earth did I say that? Because he's not, never has been, for the Portuguese, José. No, Africa, Angola, is for the Africans. He's followed for years the movements of the MPLA, their attacks on soldiers in the forests of Cabinda, in other places in the interior. Far, far away. 'But anyway, we can stay when independence comes, if independence does come,' he manages. 'Who says we have to leave? And Tiago's Angolan, you know. He should grow up here.'

Sometimes Helena can't really believe what she's hearing. Can't understand how somebody so intelligent, somebody who puts so much importance on words, can say such stupid things. 'Huuuh,' she sees the surprise on her own face. 'So you think they'll just let us stay? We come here, take over their country for four hundred years, and you think they're going to beg us not to go after independence? You think they'll just forget about the slaves and the land, the native tax, the dogs we set on them, everything we did? You think so?'

'*We* did? What do you mean, we did?' José looks shocked. 'We haven't done anything, Helena. Only came here to work, to make a living. We don't want to take anything from these people. And anyway, it's not like that here. Lots of the whites want to see an independent Angola. They're not Portuguese, they're Angolan. You know that.' He waits for her reply but she says nothing. 'It's not just about white or black, Helena. Look at Luanda; such a mixture of people. They're not going to tell us to go. Things would fall apart. No, we can stay, stay and build a new future, a new Angola, with them.'

'You sound like you're talking Portuguese propaganda now, José,' Helena sounds disdainful. '*O lusotropicalismo*, tut, tut, tut, tut! As if we're all one big happy family in Angola. Think we're all going to walk off into the sunset together?' He makes no response. 'If I was Angolan I wouldn't be turning around and thanking us for what we'd done,' she goes on. 'And anyway, they say there's going to be fighting between the different rebel factions. I mean, who's going to take over: the MPLA, the FNLA?'

'Ó Helena, we'll cross that bridge when we come to it,' José shakes his head as if all of this is hundreds of years away. 'Let's just see what happens. I really don't want to go back.' He gets up, walks to the mirror and puts his hand on her shoulder. 'Okay?' She remains silent. 'I'm going to take a bath now. Okay? Then we can have some lunch, no?' He scratches the back of his head in silence.

20

Luanda: January 2007

'*SIM*, IT'S MY LITTLE GARDEN, my little oasis,' Solange said the following evening as she lifted the pot of water and poured a little of it over some lavender. She took the head of a flower in her long fingers, lifted it to her nose, then passed it to Ana. 'It keeps me sane, you know, coming out here. I sit here and read, relax.' Ana looked at the plants on the balcony, most of which she couldn't name, then out at a couple of dying colonial houses. Before she leaned back and stared up at the other floors of the big apartment block, festooned with washing, decked out in a string of satellite dishes.

'Lots of dishes, aren't there?' she commented as Solange came back out with more water.

She lifted her shoulders, let them fall. 'I know. If one family gets one, the rest of the neighbours in the building, on the street, all want one too, you know. Like it was with radios when I was a kid. Nobody wants to be left behind, not now.' There was a pause. 'I have a dish as well, eh? What can I say?' she smiled. 'Do you want to wait out here or sit with me while I get the dinner ready?'

'No, no, no, I'll come with you,' Ana answered.

'Are you sure? Nice sunsets from here.'

Ana looked out at the buildings before her, then down towards the bay. 'No, I'll come. I think I passed this place before,' she said as she followed Solange into the kitchen.

'Ah yeah?' Solange responded, moving towards the fridge.

'Mmm,' Ana went on, not stating exactly how wanton it had looked to her then: the flaking aquamarine paint, the air conditioners clinging to the walls, the big blue barrels of water at its base. Like something from a former, floundering Soviet republic. Solange handed her a glass bottle of Coca-Cola. Just what she needed, exactly what she'd been thinking about. How did she know?

Solange rubbed her arm. 'I've been here seven years now,' she said. 'Josefa lived here before me. I moved in when I came back from France. After I divorced Mathieu. So good to have my own place after that, you know. To get something of myself back.' She stopped speaking for a moment. 'He was nice, eh, Mathieu,' she seemed to want to qualify what she'd just said. 'And it was so sweet, so romantic at the start, but it just wasn't working at the end. That's all.'

'And he? Is he still in Paris?' Ana asked.

'Yes, he is,' said Solange. 'He has his job there. Teaches Lusophone literature at a university. He knows Angola well, eh,' she smiled, 'better than me, I sometimes think.'

'And do you still see him when you go to Paris?'

'Yes, of course,' Solange emphasised her words. 'He's a good, good friend. And I love him very much. It just didn't work out, finally. That's the way it goes. But we had more than fifteen years together, fifteen good years. We were very lucky.'

'And why didn't you have any children together?' Ana wondered out loud, regretting the bluntness of her question instantly. 'Sorry, it's none of my business,' she tried to backtrack, but it was already too late.

'No, it's fine, dear,' Solange stopped what she was doing for a moment. 'The truth is I don't know exactly why. Mathieu wasn't pushed either way. He'd come from a difficult family, you know, and wasn't so crazy about bringing another child into this world. And me, well, I suppose I wasn't that keen either. I mean, there were times when I wanted a baby, but it was never a big part of my plans. I was never one of those women who put so much emphasis on starting a family. And then after… Oh, but tell me about you,' Solange's eyes turned to Ana, 'don't you have anybody special at the moment?'

'No, no, I'm single now,' Ana replied. 'Broke up with Conor… must be what, nearly ten months already. Yes, it was March, just before St Patrick's Day.'

'He was Irish?' Solange wanted to know.

'Yes, very Irish,' Ana smiled.

'And how are the Irish men?' Solange pressed, leaving Ana to think for a moment as she took two pieces of steak from the fridge.

'Complicated… ' she finally managed, trying to slow her thoughts down and verbalise properly what she wanted to say, instead of just rattling off the same old clichés. 'It's hard to know exactly what they mean, what they are saying, and if it's all just charm.' Ana stalled. 'But gentle. I mean, they're not very sophisticated or anything like that but they're not as macho as the Portuguese guys.'

'And they don't go around holding their balls in their hands like the Angolan men?' Solange wanted to know. 'You notice that, eh? Like they have a prize or something they're showing off.'

'No, no, no,' Ana said, but then she thought of something. 'Actually, the kids have started doing that, the teen-agers. Hands down their sports pants like they're American rappers or I don't know what.'

'*Idiotas*,' Solange laughed deeply. 'Like the boys here. Think they're men before they're out of nappies. Tuuuuh!'

'Please, let me do something,' Ana pleaded, not wishing to just sit there while Solange cooked her dinner, handed it to her.

'Okay, darling, okay,' Solange passed her a handful of garlic, asked her to cut it, took down an old sieve to wash the rice. 'And this Conor, why did it finish with him?' she asked a moment later, Ana thinking she liked the way her mother said the name, stressing the 'o' and 'r' at the end. The way she had said it herself for the first year of their relationship.

As Solange put a lid on the pot she considered how she should respond, knowing she could just say, I didn't want to end up like my parents, like José and Helena. 'I don't know exactly,' she began, looking around the yellow walls of the kitchen. 'There was a lot there, we really had something, you know. But there was something else missing. I mean, I loved him, loved him very much. He's a great person. And we could have gone on like that for years, forever. But...' She looked directly into Solange's deep brown eyes, keeping one of her hands on the pan where the olive oil was heating. 'I suppose I got scared. Started to feel like I was trapped, that everything was about compromise. And where's the life in that, the fun in that?' She paused, then continued, 'Oh, I was happy. I was in a way, but I could feel myself bubbling under the surface and fantasising, always fantasising about other lives I could have been living.'

She sighed and pushed the small pieces of garlic into the pan. 'I know, I know there's always compromise, that nobody gets everything in any relationship, but you can't always keep telling yourself to do the right thing, to settle. One day you'll explode.'

'It's true, it's true,' Solange nodded her head slowly, taking Ana in, what she'd just said. 'I believe every relationship is a kind of story, a tale. And you can either go along with it or not. But if you go, you have to go fully, and if you don't, then not at all. You can't always remain questioning whether it's time for staying in or getting out. You can't go on like that, life doesn't work like that.' She pushed the garlic around in the pan with a wooden spoon. 'I'll make a salad as well. You want salad, right?' Solange asked and Ana nodded.

'And have you met anybody nice here?' the older woman grinned as she turned around from the fridge a moment later: a head of green lettuce and a beef tomato cradled in one hand.

Ana considered for a split second, then thought why not, and answered Solange truthfully. 'I met a nice girl the other day,' she said. 'On Mussulo, the sister of a friend of Tiago's.'

'Ah, you like girls as well?' Solange took her in again. 'I didn't know. I've never tried it myself, but I've thought about it, really thought about it a few times.'

'Yes, it's nice,' Ana responded. 'It's nice to be with a woman sometimes.'

'Why not? Why not?' Solange agreed.

'And you, Solange? How did you meet Oscar?' Ana called out to Solange as she went into the other room, placing the meat in the pan. 'His name is Oscar, right?'

'*Sim, sim, sim*, he's called Oscar,' Solange confirmed. 'I met him one night through friends,' she reappeared in the door frame. 'At a restaurant on the Ilha. I'd seen him around before, you know. He's been here for years.'

'He's Cuban, no?'

'Yes,' Solange went over to the sink and began washing the lettuce, the tomato, sliced into them with a heavy knife. 'He came here with the other teachers in the eighties, you know, when many Cubans came to help out in the schools. When we still had something you could call schools. There were lots of Cuban troops here as well at the time, you know.'

Ana nodded. 'So, he's a teacher?' she asked.

'He *was* a teacher,' Solange corrected her. 'Not any more. He finished when they all went home, back in the early nineties.'

'And what does he do now?'

'He has a record shop, does some online music stuff,' Solange answered. 'He was the one who set up all my pages on the Internet. I'm not so good with those things. He plays in my band as well, plays guitar, you know. I sing a lot of the old *semba* songs, but with a Cuban twist, some Brazilian influence. This is what interests me.'

'Ah yeah?' Ana smiled.

'*Sim*, it's very rich, the fusion of different cultures in music. I like to see how Angola influenced their music, and see how their music can echo back into ours.'

'And Oscar, does he live here, live here with you?' Ana asked.

'*Aka!* No, no,' Solange answered. 'I prefer living alone now. Like my own space, my own bed at night. But he stays here sometimes, yes. Me at his place too. I don't want to live with him though. No, no. Don't want to live with any man. Not now.'

'And do you think he's The One?' Ana knew she was being silly, ironic.

'The One? The One? I don't know if I believe in The One. In the great love,' Solange responded, more seriously than Ana had expected. 'But we get on very well, you know. Have lots of fun. Laugh, really laugh together, for hours. And he's strong, has a strong personality. I suppose he's good for me.'

'Tell me about my father,' Ana requested a minute afterwards, as if without thinking, 'were you in love with José?' She followed Solange into the orange sitting room and began helping her move a table into the centre.

'Your father,' Solange stopped for a moment in the silence of the question, the fingers of one hand grazing her neck, the other hand on her hip. Her eyes went blank. 'I don't know, I don't honestly know, Ana. I was so young.' She stood there for a moment, then went and took a cloth from a dresser with lots of wooden sculptures on its open shelves.

'José,' she shook her head again as she turned around. 'I remember when I met him. When I was singing with Zicko. It was in one of the *musseque* clubs. Maxinde, was it Maxinde? Yes, yes. And he turned up backstage after the show. Had a friend who was a friend of Zicko's, something like that. And when I saw him I didn't think anything much of him. To me he looked as though he'd got lost, had wandered in by accident, but he was completely fascinated by the place. No, I really didn't feel anything, that first time.'

'But how, how did you end up with him if you didn't like him?' Ana wanted to know.

'*Olha*, I didn't say I didn't like him,' Solange corrected. 'It was just he didn't knock me over at first.' Ana smoothed the luminous fabric across the table. 'But I suppose I liked the attention and I must have been able to see some potential. He fancied me badly, you know. I mean, I'm not saying

I was the best-looking girl around or anything like that but I could tell he liked me, even that night. He couldn't take his eyes off me. I don't know, I suppose I thought we might have some fun together.'

Solange headed back to the kitchen to get the cutlery, the cream paper napkins, Ana following behind, taking two glasses and a bottle of water from the fridge. 'That first night he joined us for a drink and in the bar we got talking. I could tell he knew a lot about Angolan music and I liked that. He wasn't like a lot of the other white guys, just coming down to the *musseque* for a bit of a good time, you know, chasing after all the young girls. He wasn't promiscuous. I think I was the first time he'd strayed. And well, there *was* something, I suppose there *was* the seed of an attraction even that night. Oh, I don't know if it was the danger, the excitement or what, but something soon started between us,' her gaze searched out Ana.

'And did you spend... spend that first night?' Ana swallowed, asking the question as they laid the table, before heading back in the kitchen.

'No, no, no, no,' Solange shook her head as she began to put the food on the white plates. 'But I knew he wanted to, you know. And I liked that, knowing he would if I let him.' She stopped again. 'Sometimes, sometimes I think of that time, those months, as if it was a story I was writing, you know, imagining myself into, one I really got caught up in. I mean, I can actually remember sitting there, one of those nights early on, thinking of moments and scenes in the future with me in them. At the centre of them, I suppose.' She looked up again at Ana. 'It was as if it weren't entirely real, you know, any of it, so unreal I thought nobody would get hurt. You know these things we do when we're young.'

Luanda: September 1973

A WALL, A PLAIN WHITE WALL, in the blinding glare of a lamp. And against it a boy of four with a mop of mousy brown hair. Dressed in brown flares and a red jumper. Looking small, staring down at the floor, too shy to look up, out. Everything so silent, silent.

Until the music starts, the pulsating steel of the electric guitar, percussion blended into it, an instrumental of some thirty seconds, but the boy remains still, absolutely still. When all of a sudden his head jerks quickly upwards and a man's voice can be heard.

He begins to move, looking like he's done this many times before. As if he was a singer on TV or a snazzy young dude from a *musseque* club. All he's missing is the afro, a medallion maybe…

Eu tenho uma sobrinha de 6 anos de idade
I have a niece who is six years old
Também diz para mim que quer ser ye-ye
She says to me that she wants to be 'ye-ye' (hip)
Olhei pra ela, você está enganada
I looked at her: you are mistaken

você não tem idade para ser ye-ye
you are not old enough to be 'ye-ye'

He clicks his fingers to the rhythm.

Minha sobrinha, muito sorridente, olha para mim, responde assim:
My niece, all smiles, looks at me and responds:
Todo mundo disse que o tio é ye-ye
Everyone says that my uncle is ye-ye
Eu quero ser como o tio é
I want to be like my uncle

And again:

Todo mundo disse que o tio é ye-ye
Everyone says that my uncle is ye-ye
Eu quero ser como o tio é
I want to be like my uncle

Then he leans back into the air and surveys the crowd, as he embarks on the moral in his message:

Você sobrinha não siga a moda, a moda é fantasia,
a moda é ilusão
You niece, should not follow the trend; fashion is
fantasy, fashion is illusion

Warning as if he was an adult:

Você estuda para ser alguém e não ser mulher aí da rua
Study so you can be someone and not a woman of the
streets

And continues:

Ela se zanga quando lhe digo isto
She gets angry when I say this
Por isso ela disse assim para mim:
Because of that she spoke like this to me:

He shifts his shoulders to the beat.

Todo mundo disse que o tio é ye-ye
Everyone says that my uncle is ye-ye
Eu quero ser como o tio é
I want to be like my uncle

And again:

Todo mundo disse que o tio é ye-ye
Everyone says that my uncle is ye-ye
Eu quero ser como o tio é
I want to be like my uncle…

21

Luanda: January 2007

TIAGO LOOKED AT THE small white building out on the cliff overlooking the water, the tiles of its roof orange against the grey sky. He heard the blast of a horn from the jeep in front of his own. 'This is it,' he said as Ana watched Oscar's tyres come to a halt in the dust. 'You wanted to see it, didn't you, the slave museum?'

'*Sim*,' Ana confirmed, thinking this was the first of the stops on their journey south to Cabo Ledo. Off to have lunch and spend the night with Simão, a friend of Solange and Oscar's.

'So, I'm going to stay here with the girls,' Cristina told them quietly, Ana turning to see that Belita was asleep in the back and Carolina was looking wide-eyed at what was going on.

'Where are they going? Can I go?' she bleated to Cristina.

'No, no. You have to stay here and help me. Your daddy and Ana need to do something. They won't be long.'

'But help you, help you do what?' she wanted to know.

'Help me read this book, silly,' Cristina took one from her bag.

'Aw, silly, you're silly,' Carolina answered.

'Carolina,' Tiago's voice sounded stern, 'have some respect for your mother!' If only she knew what *he'd* been like, Ana thought as her espadrilles hit the ground.

'I suppose they must be inside already,' Tiago looked to see where the entrance was.

'Haven't you been here before?' Ana wondered.

'No, no,' he shook his head, 'always meant to come but never managed it. It's so out of the way, you know.' He pointed out to the water. 'That's Mussulo. You can take the boat from here as well, another way to go.' Ana looked down at the small dock, the couple of men sitting there, chewing on seeds.

'Do we have to pay anything to enter?' Tiago asked when he saw a figure in uniform standing at the door.

'No, no,' the man answered, looking from Tiago to Ana, then back again. As they went inside Solange turned and smiled, Oscar too. Come on, she seemed to be saying with a nod of her head. But Ana, as soon as she began to look around, wished she'd never suggested stopping here, as her eyes took in the sets of shackles in different sizes, the rack for stretching the human body, the rest of the instruments of torture. All she wanted was to get back out into the open.

'Luanda, millions of my people were shipped out from there, for centuries,' Ana could remember somebody telling her years before. An Angolan, it was an Angolan man she'd met in Dublin, skin black against an overcast summer morning. 'No, I never go to Portugal, never been there. I wouldn't give the Portuguese my money. If I have to go home I go through Paris or London. Portugal, no. No way.'

'There's an upstairs as well, eh?' Solange said as she and Oscar began to mount the steps, Ana going behind Tiago who'd been silent since they'd come inside. Walking up after him, she felt her stomach sink, hearing flesh tearing and women wailing, imagining a long line of human souls shackled and walking single file out of the country's interior, sold by a local chief to the Portuguese. And then she heard the voice, the voice of a woman she'd overheard at a party, 'The Portuguese aren't racists. No, no. Everybody mixed well in their colonies: blacks, whites, Indians. Not like the British, no!'

I'd love to lock her in here for a while to see what she'd say then, Ana thought, eyes resting on a branding iron. Before she thought of Brazil again, of São Salvador da Bahia, and the big women dressed in elaborate frills, shaking their big behinds.

'Two hundred *kwanzas*,' she heard the attendant say shortly afterwards, as they left the building.

'Sorry, what?' she tried to snap out of her distractions.

'Two hundred *kwanzas*. You have to pay two hundred *kwanzas*,' he repeated.

'For what?' Ana asked, Tiago at her shoulder now. 'You told us there was no entrance fee, that we didn't have to pay anything to go in.'

The man looked at Ana calmly, seriously. Lifted his finger as if he was a teacher at school explaining something. 'To enter, no, there's no charge to enter. But to leave, yes. It costs two hundred *kwanzas*, two hundred each.'

Ana didn't know whether to laugh or to get annoyed. 'Are you serious?' she asked.

'*Sim, sim…*'

'Is that right?' Solange interrupted, walking up behind the attendant. He turned around as she pulled up to her full height. 'You get out of here,' she commanded. 'I'm telling you now.'

He looked at her as if he was giving something some deep consideration, drops of sweat glinting on his forehead, before he laughed. 'Ha, ha, ha, no hard feelings.' He shook Tiago's hand, then Ana's, then Solange's. 'A man has to survive, eh?'

'Get out of it,' Solange warned again, and the last thing Ana saw was her brother slip him a couple of notes before he scurried away.

'It's really cool, no?' Tiago called out to Ana a while later, at the next stop, as she walked towards a precipice to look over the red earth of the canyon, out at the ocean beyond. 'They say it's the second biggest in the world, after the Grand Canyon.'

'Yes, it's marvellous, really marvellous,' she replied, not turning, not wanting to explain what she thought of it. And use words, always words, to describe things, feelings, when sometimes an image was enough in itself.

'It's how I imagine the moon to look,' Solange was speaking to Oscar, her voice loud, carrying on the wind. 'Sometimes I drive out here on my own, sit here for hours.'

'You never told me that,' Oscar laughed.

'Oh darling, there's a lot I haven't told you,' Solange teased. '*Olha* Ana, you want me to take a photo of you there?' she called.

'Yes, I'd love that,' Ana unwound the string of her camera from her wrist. Handed it to Solange, before she moved back out to the edge of the precipice.

'Like that, like that,' Solange instructed, pressing the shutter as Ana turned, the lower half of her body still facing the water. She repeated the pose as Solange took another shot. 'Let me get another one,' she insisted, crouching down on one knee. '*Sim, sim*, that's it. *Beleza*, beautiful,' Solange smiled from behind the camera. 'I adore your dress, Ana. It's so elegant.' Ana looked down at the navy and white striped number that flowed out into a full skirt, her waist accentuated by a red belt. Smiled as she played with the pearls on her neck for a moment. Thinking of Tiago raising his eyebrows, silently telling the woman not to encourage her.

'Come on, Solange, let's get one together,' Ana called out. 'That's true, we don't have a photo of the two of us,' she cheered. '*¿Oscar, puedes hacer un fotito de nosotras, por favor?*' Ana asked her mother's partner in Spanish to take a little photo of them, enjoying the way the language rolled off her tongue, the fun she could have with it. Like when she was talking to her Spanish friends in Dublin, sitting smoking and drinking after mounds of food. '*¡Claro, guapa!*' Oscar took the camera from Solange, Ana smiling at the self-conscious flirtation in his tone, thinking she liked him, liked him very much.

'Okay,' he said as Solange went up to Ana and put her arm around her shoulder, Ana sliding a hand around her mother's waist. There was a click. Then another and another. 'And just one more,' he insisted, playing with the small device, taking two or three more as it turned out. Leaving Ana to wait, breathing in the scent of coconut off her mother, feeling the touch of her fingers on her upper arm. Almost nestling her head into the other woman's collarbone, stopping only at the last moment.

'They're beautiful,' Oscar said, holding out the camera as the two women came towards him, 'look.' Ana looked at his dark eyes, then down at the small screen as Solange took it in her hand. Moved from the first image to the last. Slowly, then more quickly, until it seemed as though they were moving in a film, each image ever so slightly different to the last. Solange laughed, looking proud, like she'd just come up with a new invention, Ana wondering that she'd never seen this done before.

Luanda: April 1974

IT'S SIX, MUST BE AROUND SIX in the morning when José's eyes jolt open. He feels a hand on his shoulder, shaking him, 'Wake up, wake up!' He looks at the fingers, follows them the length of an arm and sees Helena standing over him. What the hell? he thinks to himself, remembering it was late when he went to bed the night before, that he still has another half an hour of sleep if he wants. He thinks of grumbling, but says nothing, just turns over to the sound of Tiago's voice calling to him from the door. 'Daddy, Daddy, wake up!'

Helena leaves and comes back a moment later with the transistor radio. 'José, listen! They've taken over the radio stations, the airport. The army have called a coup.' He jolts up, takes the radio from her hand. 'They made another announcement a few minutes ago. They think it's going to be…'

'Where? Here, in Luanda? The MPLA?' he doesn't understand.

'No, no, no, in Lisbon. They're saying, they're saying…'

'Ssssh,' he quietens her, tries to hear what the announcer is saying, to make out what station it is – Rádio Clube Português.

But there's nothing, no announcements now, just music being played like any other morning. So he turns the dial, desperate to find out what the others have to say, thinking he'll try the BBC World Service, see if it has made their news. But then the phone rings and his heart stops for a moment. 'Yes?' he picks up the Bakelite receiver, hears Bruno's voice. Bruno from work, who's been in Angola for generations and has been waiting for this day ever since.

'Yes, they say it started just after midnight,' only Bruno's voice, his end of the conversation, is audible now. 'They played "Grândola, Vila Morena". You know, Zeca Afonso. Yes, that was the signal, yes. The song was banned. No, I don't know much more but this is the end, definitely the end. Caetano is finished. The army have taken over. Come to Horácio's place later. Bring Helena and Tiago. Sure, sure. *Adeus, camarada,*' he hangs up.

Leaving José with a buzzing in his ear, not sure what to do: whether to get washed and dressed, phone his parents in Lisbon, head straight to Horácio's, or just stay right here, exactly where he is, in case there is any more news.

In the end the three of them move into the sitting room, arranging themselves around the polished mahogany stereo system, staying there right on into the afternoon. Wondering if there will be lots of bloodshed and not quite comprehending that there has been so little so far, that all of this has passed off almost entirely peacefully. Listening as the Portuguese public rush out onto the streets of Lisbon, flooding the place with their hopes for the future. As carnations, red carnations, are passed out at the flower market. Until they're everywhere, bright red against the April grey, the green of the soldiers' uniforms.

And later, that evening, sitting in Horácio's, the lounge

all desaturated, washed out tones, José takes Helena's hand in his, tears in his eyes. Wanting to say, though he can't quite, that they've made it, finally made it, that this is the start of a whole new beginning. That Angola will be independent, and Mozambique and Cape Verde and Portugal will never again be in the hands of the Fascists, the PIDE put to an end. Pigs, they should be strung up, every last one of them, he thinks.

But where he sees a new beginning, Helena only knows this is an end. And that before too long they will most likely have left Angola. Be back in Lisbon, or Oporto. Like the rest of the Portuguese here, she thinks, resigned to the fact. Feeling her heart thud and eyes widen as she watches José. Because he believes, truly believes, everything is going to be okay. While it's left to her to figure out just what they're going to do now.

22

Cabo Ledo: January 2007

'AND YOU'LL HAVE SOME SQUID AS WELL?' all eyes were on Ana, later that day, as the host Simão put a big slab of white meat on the plate.

'If that doesn't kill her, I don't know what will,' Solange laughed, smoking a cigarette out of the side of her mouth, exhaling towards the sand and away from the table. 'She might put a few pounds on, eh?' Tiago laughed as Ana felt her cheeks burn.

'It's true, eh? Your sister, she's very thin,' a man, whose name Ana couldn't remember, commented.

'*Olha*, let the girl eat in peace,' Solange instructed, her saviour suddenly, while Ana stared down at the plate, blushing even more now.

'Who wants another *pinxo*?' Simão turned to the barbecue then back to the table, a tray of pork and vegetable skewers in one hand.

'I'll go for one,' Tiago affirmed.

'Me too,' said Cristina.

'Mammy, I want one. I want one,' Carolina was eyeing the tray up.

'No, no, no, I'll share mine with you,' Cristina was firm.

Told Carolina not to even think of sulking as she flopped back down in her plastic chair.

'Ana, you don't need one, do you, he, he, he, he?' Simão's laugh was hearty, as he went to the end of the table and gave one to his cousin.

'No, no thanks,' she said politely, feeling stupid as soon as the words were out because he'd only been joking and she'd answered in earnest.

She lifted a bottle of wine, looked around to see if anybody else needed a top-up. Saw one or two glasses were empty or half-empty and began to ask who was for more, then decided she didn't want to draw any more attention to herself. Because she was feeling the way she did when she sometimes got caught in front of the projector lights in a lecture: exposed, fraudulent, faltering. A lot of them are drinking beer anyway, she cast a sideways glance along the table and put the wine back down, her mind racing.

'And Paris, are you going to Paris again soon?' she heard Tiago's voice. Though it took her a moment to understand it was Solange he was speaking to, Solange he was asking about Paris.

'End of the month,' Solange answered, her red headscarf radiant against the sky. 'The first gig is there in early February. Then we set off for the south of France. Back up and into Belgium, Holland. Then Paris again.'

'Do you like it there, in Paris?' Cristina wanted to know, all conversation at this end of the table focused on Solange now.

'Eh, I adore Paris. Who doesn't?' she smiled. 'Such beautiful buildings, the galleries, the Seine. I love it. And the cafés, so sophisticated, you know. I have one I go to all the time, the Café de Flore. It's on the Boulevard Saint-Germain.

The hot chocolate is amazing.'

Ana could see the café on that cold December morning she'd trekked there with Conor, and that photo with her in it, the two men sitting outside, smiling at her pose. The Café de Flore, where she'd imagined herself for a year of her youth at least, sitting watching Simone and Sartre at work, writing in her own journal, head lifting only now and then when the door opened and the bitter wind crept in. The Café de Flore, she thought again, trying, but not quite managing, to imagine Solange there.

'And the French, how do you like the French?' Tiago was interested to know what Solange thought.

She smiled and shrugged her shoulders dramatically in response. '*Je ne sais pas.*' The others laughed at her imitation of French malaise. 'No, no, no, they're okay. I mean, I have a lot of friends there. But they're not open. They're not like us Africans, you know. Much more closed. Much more about themselves.'

'And superior, they think of themselves as superior to us, no? That's what my friend Mbaxi says,' a skinny guy around Ana's age gave his five cents on the topic from down the table. 'He's lived there for nearly ten years now. Says it was very hard to get on, to get started.'

Solange didn't say anything for a moment, seemed to be considering something before she responded. She lowered her voice, 'Listen, I don't normally like to talk about these things, but if you ask me I think all whites believe they are superior in a way, whether it's in France or Portugal or the States. They still have that attitude, you know, even after all this time, even after everything that's happened. It's incredible. You have to laugh at it; otherwise it would drive you crazy. But the truth is they just can't imagine that other people see the world differently, that Africans don't see it the way they do. That our reality, our way of being in this world, is different. Sorry, eh. No offence.' Solange looked at Tiago, at Cristina, and for a moment her eyes rested on Ana.

'And then when they like us they try and make exotic birds of us, you know,' she was on a roll now. 'I mean, some of the things the record company in Paris wanted me to do! Asking me to sing barefoot like Cesaria. Or to wear this dress, that dress, who knows what. And the journalists, any ones I've met, they're always looking for some angle about the war, horror stories. Was I with the MPLA or UNITA? Did I see any fighting? Did I lose any family? As if that's all there was to say about my country.' The young guy was nodding his head. 'I mean, I played along with it at the start, wore what they wanted me to, said what they wanted to hear and then I thought, forget this, I'm no clown for no white man.' Ana looked at her scarf again, the big hoops in her ears.

'And do you ever play much in Portugal?' Tiago wondered, pushing his sunglasses up his nose.

'Ah, I have a few concerts there later in the year, in summer, you know. Outdoor stuff, in Lisbon, in the Algarve. After Spain. We'll see how they go.' She stopped speaking, looked down to the water, then back at the table. 'It will be nice to go there. I like it. I've sung there a few times. Backing stuff; with some big names.' Solange smiled, as Ana wondered if she was waiting for somebody to ask who these famous musicians were. She herself said nothing, too busy picturing Solange singing, singing out to the river, the ocean, in Lisbon.

And this is what she was still thinking about, hours afterwards, when the singing began. As Oscar tuned his guitar, before Solange stood beside his chair, hand on her stomach, singing; sweet but strong, '*Muxima Oh! Oh! Muxima Oh! Oh! Muxima,*' notes carrying on the breeze. So beautiful the way she sang, so tender. *A minha mãe é linda.*

A smirk crossed Ana's face as she turned her back to the woman and poured herself another Cutty Sark, watched as the Coca-Cola spilled on the tablecloth. She thought of getting a cloth to wipe it, then figured what the hell. 'Bravo,' she clapped a few minutes later when Solange finished. Then turned to Daniel, Simão's cousin. 'You sing yourself?' she asked.

'Oh no, not me!'

'Aw, come on, you must know some songs. At least one.' Solange had started singing again. 'Come on, come on, Daniel, come on, Simão, let's all sing a tune together,' she badgered the two men, then suddenly broke into an old *fado* herself, singing over Solange.

And as she sang she became aware that Tiago was watching her. 'Ana, Ana, take it easy,' she heard him say to her.

But she sang on and on, as if oblivious to his words, only halting her tune when she saw everybody was looking in her direction. 'Why, Tiago?' she demanded. 'Why do you want me to stop?' she threw her brother a look. 'So we can all listen to how great she is, the big star?' she indicated Solange with a cock of her head.

'Ana, please,' there was a hint of desperation in Tiago's tone now. 'Relax, just relax.'

'Just fuck off and leave me alone, will you, Tiago,' Ana responded, and began singing again.

'Ana,' Solange's voice could be heard now, 'Ana, what's wrong with you? Are you all right? Calm down, please. Everything's okay.'

Ana turned and looked at her mother then, held her down with her eyes like an insect she was about to dissect, before she said it, couldn't believe she was saying it. 'You! You can go and fuck yourself too!'

Until the next thing she knew she was stumbling along the beach, beneath a vast moon. Certain now that her growing suspicions had been correct. That Solange really was nothing but artifice. An act to the last note gliding through the air. With everybody hanging on her words. Her pretty words, her sweet way of singing a tune, but what was the truth of this woman, her mother? Mythmaker, sly snake of a charmer.

She'd left Ana, let her go, abandoned her to José and Helena. Though what stung, stung most, was the fact that she had been to Portugal, been there many times, and never come to see her. This casual mention of the country and Ana's own cringe of a memory; looking out over the railway tracks and down towards the beach before she went to bed, sure her mother was out there somewhere. That the ocean would keep them connected and she'd walk up from it, out of it, one day. Come and watch over her when she wasn't aware of it, least expected it.

But this would be no *Stella Dallas*, no mother outside the window of her daughter's wedding, looking in. What were they now but two women with nothing more than a sleazy story between them? And one of them, thirty years later, proud as punch with all eyes fixed on her. Oh, she loved an audience all right, Solange, would do anything for her audience.

Ana noticed the huts on the hillside, lights from one or two of them, and moved on, power in her step, a sweet revenge in her drunken stumble. Putting her shoulders back as she passed a couple of fishermen sitting by their boats drinking beer. Laugh, did one of them just laugh at me? she paused for a moment and spat a look at the shadows, then told herself to let them be, let them laugh at her for all she cared. Stupid fools!

She noticed only then that Solange was trying to catch up with her. '*Olha*, Ana, wait, wait a minute. Talk to me. Please,' she called out, but Ana only ignored her, attempted to move more quickly. '*Olha*, you can't go on like this! Get a hold of yourself, Ana,' the voice was strong, sure of itself, angry suddenly. Making Ana feel small, silly, as if she was about to topple over for a moment. 'Who do you think you are, Ana? Can't talk like an adult? Acting like some kind of brat stomping off like that. Oh, what has he taught you, that father of yours?' Solange went on.

And it was those words that made Ana gather her strength again, caused her to turn and march up to the woman's face. Thinking if she were a man, and Solange too, then she'd hit her, smack her one in the jaw. 'Who do I think I am? Who do I think I am?' some vein of madness, explosion of feelings; a voracious emergence of a silent, wild part of her told her to go on, to continue. To release it all.

'No, who the hell do *you* think you are?' Ana hissed. 'Who do you think you're fooling with your voice, your persona? "Oh look at Solange; so sensitive, so fine the way she sings." But you're full of lies, all lies. You don't live as you sing, Solange. I know, I know that. Everything is performance with you, no? Everything for the show, isn't it. Isn't it?'

Solange stared back at her as though she was going to meet her hateful word for hateful word, until she seemed to stop and think again. 'That's it, daughter, that's the way,' her arms were outstretched, before she put her hands on her hips, voice calm, sure of itself, leaving Ana lost for words for a few seconds. 'Just let it out, let it out! There's been something up with you all day, so take it out on me if you want. Come on, come on!'

Twisting, she's twisting things, Ana could see clearly how Solange was manipulating another situation. Trying to turn the tables on her. She felt a swift drop of breath behind her ribcage as she turned to walk away. Deciding there was nothing for it now but to opt out of this charade of a reconciliation, because she'd only been fooling herself these last few days, hadn't she? Trying her best to make her mother love her, charming her into it. Thinking Solange was going to make her whole, as if it was suddenly all going to make sense.

Luanda: July 1974

JOSÉ DRIVES TO THE *MUSSEQUE* CLUB. Through the streets of a city thousands are already planning to leave. Going to meet Ricardo, Horácio or one of the young writers or musicians he is friends with.

He parks his car and walks slowly down the steps into the dimly lit space, the music starting up with the movement of his feet; the strains of the cello, the violin, Samuel Barber's *Adagio for Strings*. And hearing the tune, he moves towards the bar, looking around for his friends. Only it's not Barber's composition that reaches him, but the music of the band on stage: various sets of drums, guitars, congas. And a deep, smooth voice grooving down onto the beat, making more than half the place hit the floor already.

But still it takes him a moment to make her out; the tall figure on stage in her *pano*, next to the other backing singer, brown palm leaves on burnt yellow, a scarf of the same pattern wound around her head. Getting into it, really getting down into it, throwing her arms out, then turning and wiggling her behind at the audience before revolving around into a *semba* stance, one hand on her stomach, the other holding on to the microphone. As Barber's movement continues to rise.

And it's then he stops, stops right where he is standing, José, and leans against a pillar. Looking at her breasts, the bracelets on her arms and wrists, with the violins and cello rising, growing stronger as she moves her body: frenetically, deliciously.

Until the beat up on stage slows, slackens, Barber's composition rising again, and she looks down, looks over at him, seems to smile, a big warm smile. And already, already he thinks he knows her...

23

The River Kuanza: January 2007

'I STILL CAN'T BELIEVE THIS PLACE is closed,' said Solange as they got out of the car at the abandoned resort on the River Kuanza. 'We used to come here all the time.' They began walking along a path. 'Oscar saw a crocodile there, right there, the last time we stayed here,' Solange pointed a minute later. 'We'd gone out together, to have dinner over at the restaurant, but he'd gone back to get something, a present for me. It was my birthday. He'd just slipped back to our room for a minute but when he came out there was the crocodile looking at him, just staring up at him.'

'And wasn't he terrified? What did he do?' Ana asked as Solange laughed.

'He just got to the restaurant as quickly as he could.'

'Otherwise the crocodile might have been eating *him* for dinner,' said Ana.

'That's right. And Oscar had a belly then. Would have made a fine meal for a crocodile.' Solange paused. 'But no, you see them now and then here. It's not that unusual,' she looked around. 'I still can't believe the state it's in.'

They continued moving around the complex, strolling towards the river, past cream and peach buildings all closed up. Ana wondered when they were going to talk about the previous night, about her outburst, the scene she'd caused. After all, wasn't that why they were making the journey back to Luanda together? Why Ana and Oscar had swapped places? But she was still too ashamed, too timid, to broach the topic. Perhaps they could just leave it, she thought, let the afternoon linger on and speak about it another day.

Another day when she wasn't so deathly hung over, with a stomach full of fear and hysteria. Feeling as if she'd been reduced to her elements, the bare bones of herself. So out of synch with the world, letting everything slip behind her vacant eyes, her painted lips. Paralysed now by uncertainty, like those mornings in Dublin when she got stuck in front of the mirror, wondering if she actually was one of those freaks who wandered the city's streets. That quiver of a terrible thought that she wasn't among the watchers, no, never had been. That she, she was among the watched.

'You know, I didn't know they were taking you to Portugal,' it was Solange who finally spoke. 'Everything happened so quickly, you know. They were staying here, were going to sit things out, like José wanted. They were going to raise you, but I still saw you, visited you every week. *A minha filha.*' Ana looked at Solange.

'But then the 27th of May happened, and Zicko was murdered. And me, I was off to France but really I didn't know what I was doing. Was terrified,' Solange looked away. 'But I went to see you, went to see you a few mornings after they took Zicko, and the four of you were gone. The whole place was like the *Titanic*. Like the scene of a crime. Most of the clothes still there, all your father's books, all the dishes. And for a moment I was sure you had all been killed. Killed or taken away during the night. It was terrible, terrible in Luanda during those days.'

Ana watched the scene unfold as Solange spoke. 'But then when I looked around a bit more I could see there hadn't been any kind of a fight,' she continued. 'And I remembered your father's typewriter, his blue Valentine typewriter. I went to the office, looked at his desk and it was gone. So I knew they must have gone back to Portugal. There was no way your father would have been allowed to keep the typewriter if they'd been taken by the soldiers. And there was no way your father would have left without it.'

'But why, why didn't they tell you they were leaving? Get word to you?' Ana could feel the confusion, the anger, rising in her voice as she turned to Solange.

Who shook her head again. 'Maybe they thought I'd been killed with Zicko. It was a chaotic time, Ana. Horrific. Nobody knew what was going to happen next,' Solange sighed, ran a hand along her upper arm. 'Maybe the attempted coup was the last straw for them; they'd had enough of all the violence, the fear, the insecurity. Somebody must have got them airline tickets and they just fled. Went to the airport as quickly as they could.'

'Leaving you on your own?' Ana looked at Solange.

Who returned the gaze. 'Yes, they left me here on my own. They took you without telling me.'

As the two women looked at one another Ana remembered something, how Helena had sometimes insinuated that Solange was manipulative, was clever, that she would only try and turn Ana against her parents if she ever met her. And here she was now, focusing on what her father and Helena had done, instead of owning up to her own actions. Ana thought of something, but told herself to say nothing, then changed her mind just as suddenly and spoke. 'Why did you come and see me that morning? Were you going to take me to Paris with you?'

Solange's face fell as she struggled to find the words. 'I… I don't know. I suppose I just went to say goodbye, thought you'd be still here in Angola when I came back. I never planned to stay in Paris for long, but then you were gone and oh…'

'But why didn't you come to Lisbon, come and find me?' Ana watched the question register quickly on Solange's face. 'Why didn't you go there and find me, raise me with you? You had family there, no?' she put the questions to the woman calmly. Not interested in hurting her, in extracting payment for time deferred, not now, not today, but wanting to know what she would say.

Because she would understand, could take it, if Solange admitted that besides the pressure of her family, and not having a place of her own, or a husband, she had also seen this baby as a burden. As something that would hold her back, stall her career, mean the only singing she would do for the next few years would be into a cradle: 'Hush little baby, don't say a word…'

'But it was difficult, so difficult back then,' Solange took some time to think before she answered, her profile framed by the water, silver hoop earring moving slightly in the breeze. 'My family didn't even know I'd had you, besides Josefa. I couldn't just leave and go to Lisbon: no job, nothing. And I didn't think they would just hand you back, you know, José and Helena. They really loved you.' There was another pause. 'Oh, I thought about it, thought about it all the time. It was really a hell, really,' she took Ana in with her eyes. 'I fell apart those first couple of years in Paris. Try to understand. It felt as though I'd lost everything, couldn't go on. My life was a mess. But I knew, knew you'd have more opportunities in life, more of a chance with them, and I didn't want to confuse you, to hurt you. I wanted you to have a normal life there. Still I thought of you every day, Ana, believe me! Birthdays, Christmas. All the days of my life since I brought you into this world.'

She wouldn't say it, still wouldn't say it, Ana knew, as she watched reality unfold, wondering if this was exactly how it had all happened.

Outside Luanda: July 1974

THEIR FIRST NIGHT TOGETHER, José and Solange. Dinner and a room at an old colonial hotel outside the city, the setting, their clothes all saturated tones. He's told Helena he has to go to Benguela for work, that he'll see her the following evening. Couldn't believe how calm he was, how easy lying to her came in the end. He wonders that he's never done this before, that people don't do it more often. But maybe they do. Anyway, this isn't some cheap infidelity, what has started with Solange. Beautiful, funny, clever Solange, sitting opposite him in a yellow mini-dress, hair afro-style.

Solange who smiles, can't seem to stop smiling, as he kisses her in the room later. Because he amuses her, her lover. Yes, that's what he is, her lover. Looking so intense, so serious, his movements delicate, gentle, even though he can't wait to put himself inside her. It's as if, as if he thinks she's some kind of rare flower he has to handle with care, while she watches the whole scene as if she were outside her own body, with an aerial view of events.

And he, José, he has never felt this for someone before. The quivering of his heart when they speak on the telephone, the wildness of the scene when he pulls up and she gets into his car, a safe enough distance from both their homes. And this sense that he's found what he's been looking for, who he's been waiting for. Even if she is ten years younger, but anyway. She's grown up, so much more mature than he expected, and every time they meet she surprises him with something new. Yes, he's sure, sure of Solange.

And she, what she's sure of is that she's been expecting an adventure like this for years. Her desire rising like humidity in a hothouse as she catches herself reflected in the hunger of his eyes. As she pulls him towards her, onto her, dreaming of poets and films and so many places she has never been.

24

Luanda: January 2007

SO A WEEK, JUST A WEEK LEFT in Angola. Or not even. Friday morning Ana would be in the airport, back in a wintery Lisbon that same evening. 'This is just going to be a regular week,' Cristina had said, sighing with relief or stress, Ana couldn't tell, saying that the girls were going back to school. And Tiago had left for work that morning; looking sheepish and gloomy late the night before when Ana had finally arrived home. Greeting her sideways while he kept his eyes on the TV, saying nothing about her long drive from Cabo Ledo with Solange.

She scratched a mosquito bite on her knuckle, wondering if she should have another cigarette or go back inside. Sit down and talk with Tiago, or go to her room and get on with her book. Because there wasn't that much time left, was there? She'd be back teaching the following week, back working on her PhD, and somehow she still hadn't managed to get through all the reading she'd brought with her. The book on post-classical Hollywood remained only half-finished and that book on colour in film, she'd flicked through it again and again, a paragraph glanced at here and there, but still hadn't read it properly. Yes, she really needed to focus, get back to *Desperately Seeking Susan* instead of desperately seeking Solange.

She thought again about Saturday night, that swift, violent break with her newly-found mother. That turning away, that kick in the face, crawling back to her tent. She lit another cigarette, felt her insides tremble, then soothed herself, remembered everything was okay. Yesterday, yesterday sorted all of that out, she told herself. Or, maybe not yesterday but this morning, this afternoon.

All day she'd sifted through Solange's words: first at home, then in the Portuguese café, and on into her slow stroll down to the Marginal. Trying to decide for herself what was true and what was not. Or might not be, exactly. Putting the story together, the scenes in order, discarding what was superfluous and trying to get to the core of what had happened. How it had looked from the outside, felt from the inside. But understanding, somewhere between the bay and that map of the world on the wall of the university, that she didn't have to be involved in any of this, not if she didn't want to. In these stories and contradictions, claims and counter-claims. Because that was all to do with them, with José and Solange, Helena as well. Dancing with death in a different Angola, flickering fragments of a lost world, a vanished time. She could only change the future.

And now, for the first time in a couple of weeks, she could feel the pull of her house in Dublin. That place in The Tenters; so small, so quaint, nestled in the grey-green silence of her road. Not far from town, no great distance from the hustle, bustle, blaring of car horns and rumble of buses along a sodden George's Street, but so peaceful still. Her bedroom with all her winter coats and shoes. Her own bed. And tea with Lenny, tea and dark chocolate Digestives

while the wind whistled outside, early on in a late November week. Soon the older neighbours would be saying, 'You
can see the stretch in the evenings already,' counting down
the days to the start of the second half of the year when they
could begin commenting, 'You can see the nights drawing
in already.'

Ana looked down towards the voices coming from the
back of the apartment building, then out at the city again.
Glad to have her strength back, herself back, and not feel as
weak, as mad, as she had the day before. Tiago walked out
then. 'Do you have a light?' he asked as he rustled open a
pack of cigarettes.

'Of course,' she sparked her flame and watched the tip
of his cigarette glow orange, her mind moving from yesterday to today, tonight. 'How did work go?' she asked.

'Phew!' he sighed. 'Work, you know. They fired a few
people. Were caught stealing over Christmas. Walking out
the door with computers and stereos under their arms like
Santa had just arrived.'

'Are you serious?'

'Yeah, happens all the time,' Tiago nodded. 'People
taking what they want. It's difficult here, you know. Complicated, trying to run a business. People rob all the time.'

Ana thought for a moment. 'I guess if it's happening
from the top down in the country it isn't going to stop any
time soon.'

'You're right, you're right,' he exhaled, rubbing his left
eye, yawning, trying to suppress it, 'sometimes I wonder if
there's any hope for this place.' He looked out at the buildings before him. 'And how did it go? With Solange? Yesterday?' he asked tentatively.

'Fine, fine,' Ana answered, wondering what to leave

in, what to take out. 'I'm just glad she didn't walk away, you know. I was so angry with her on Saturday night,' she looked down at her shoes.

'That's normal, it's usual,' Tiago consoled. 'Don't worry about that now.'

'No, I suppose you're right,' she replied, 'but I don't like it when I'm like that.' There was a silence. 'No, it went okay,' she went on, 'helped me to understand her story a bit more: the pressure she was under, how conservative her family was. Her dad was so strict, he would have killed her if he'd found out she'd gotten pregnant by a married *tuga*. Maybe killed José as well,' she laughed. 'Oh, I still don't know, I still have a lot of questions but these things are always complicated, aren't they? They're never simple.' Tiago nodded his head in agreement.

Ana brushed a fly from her thigh, looking at the khaki-coloured hot pants she was wearing, then towards the Cuca building and the city streets where she could see herself wandering earlier that day. 'But there's something I still really can't understand,' she said. 'That I don't think I'll ever get.'

'And what is that?' Tiago asked, skin glowing against his white shirt with the red stripes, still looking fresh despite the hour.

Ana considered for a moment if she should say what she was thinking, then thought why not, enough had been said in these last few days, left unsaid over the years. 'It's Helena. I still don't get why she would raise another woman's child. I mean, I know she always wanted more children and couldn't have them, but still... I mean, how many women would raise a child their husband had with another woman?'

The flicker of a look on Tiago's face, Ana was sure she was imagining it, before he began to speak. 'Helena, Helena was no angel herself, you know, Ana.'

'What do you mean? What are you talking about?' she wondered.

'Oh, maybe I got it all wrong,' Tiago rubbed his eye again. 'But I met somebody here, a man from Oporto, a few months ago. He knew Helena, you know, asked me how she was, and when I told him she'd died he just broke down, broke down completely. Started wailing like a child.'

Ana lit another cigarette, listening carefully to her brother. 'Anyway, this guy, this Eduardo, he insisted I go for dinner with him, bought me drink after drink all night. *Olha*, I didn't want to be there, had never seen this guy in my life, but I couldn't just leave him. He spoke all night about Helena, about how he had bumped into her here years before.' Tiago looked at Ana. 'Oh, maybe he didn't know what he was saying, he was pretty drunk, you know. Or maybe I just got it wrong,' Tiago paused again, 'but…'

Luanda: August 1971

BACK, BACK IN TIME, before the revolution, before Solange, and Helena again. A *cacimbo* morning, slipping out of the apartment, the red of her silk headscarf bright against the mist, wondering what the neighbours would say if they could see her now.

Months, yes, it must be months since he's shown any interest in her, José, all sexual excitement channelled into his work, the big throbbing phallus of his ego taking on far too many projects, then feeling like a superhero when he manages, just barely, to get them all done. If he doesn't have a breakdown in the meantime, that is. But that's all part of it, isn't it? What he gets off on.

And she, she's supposed to pat him on the back, rub his feet and make his dinner. Shake her head and think, God, it must be tough being a man. Pretend she doesn't see his eyes fixating on those pretty African women. While she's stuck at home with Tiago, all the days dripping into one another, nobody else for company. It wasn't supposed to be like this, was it? Their generation was going to be different; women burning their bras, rocking the establishment like poor young Janis Joplin. But still it's the men who go out into the world to seek their glory, the women forgotten at home.

And perhaps she wouldn't mind, wouldn't be so resentful, if he didn't expect her to jump at the chance of spending an afternoon, an evening with him, the odd time he *is* free. Like she should be grateful, as if it were some kind of a gift, a few hours with her husband. Lunch on the Ilha, a movie at the local cinema or dinner with friends. But it all seems so stale now, somehow so contrived.

And that's how she feels when Eduardo first turns up in April. When she catches sight of him one sweltering morning as she's out pushing Tiago in his pram. At first she can't quite believe it's him. Eduardo with the blue eyes who used to wander down from the hills of Oporto to walk her out along the river, the mist rolling in from the sea. Eduardo who has been in Nova Lisboa for years but is here in Luanda just for a few days. And who looks so surprised as he takes her and the baby in, telling her that she hasn't changed one bit.

But maybe that wasn't the way it was at all. Perhaps the scenes are in black and white and there are a few freckles sprinkled across the pale skin of Helena's nose. And she still looks incredibly young and pretty, slim in her grey skirt and fitted white blouse, a small navy scarf tied around her neck. Not really knowing what she's doing, but still not half as innocent as she looks.

Even if it's true he took her by surprise, Eduardo, when he turned up in Luanda. This teenage sweetheart who went to Angola after school to fight, just another lamb put to slaughter on the Portuguese altar. Only to fall in love with the country's green landscapes, its giant orchids, the bright buildings of Nova Lisboa. Where he returns to help an uncle and aunt run their café, deciding to settle there himself.

Only hearing later, years later, that she is living in Angola too. Helena Fonseca from Oporto.

And when they do finally meet, it's only months later that anything happens. An afternoon when they're sitting beneath a coconut tree with Tiago asleep in his pram, shaded from the sun. Talking about a film they've both seen, laughing at one another's stories. Not mentioning their respective spouses. Just excited, both of them, because they've slipped so easily back into one another's company, have found one another again. They always took it for granted, when they were teenagers, that they would settle down, end up together.

But life hasn't turned out that way. Has only got more complicated, not easier, as time has gone on. Leaving Helena wondering, in the silence of a young mother's afternoon, what relationships really are. If they're about your feelings, theirs, or both, coupled with whatever unknowable ingredients are between you. Or if they are just stories you make up as you go along, have to stick with until the end once you've started them. God, she's tired of her own one now. Is sick of feeling nothing, nothing for José, as if the colour has been slowly stolen from their life. And that's why she leans in towards Eduardo, moves slowly in towards his blue, blue eyes from home.

25

Mussulo: January 2007

THE BACK OF A HAND brushing grains of sand from a
behind, the skin of the palm much lighter than the rich tones
of the buttock, the jade of the bikini bottoms. Solange turned
towards Ana, wrapping the sarong around her waist. 'Are
you ready, darling?'

'Yes, yes, just a moment,' Ana replied as she replaced her
bookmark between pages turning yellow, going grey, and
stood up. Rubbing her legs and looking at the mock Rudi
Gernreich 'below-the-navel' swimsuit she was wearing,
sliding her flip-flops between her toes and thinking that it
was heels, heels that would really go with this outfit. She let
the loose cheesecloth dress fall over her head, fixed a long,
thin yellow scarf around her waist and pushed her hair back
from her face.

All the while moving from glimpses of herself to curious
glances at Solange, wondering what she would look like
onscreen. Thinking, yes, she'd probably turn out well on
celluloid, the camera picking up the bright colours she
wore, her tall, slender figure filling up the frame, her face
always so full of whatever she was feeling. Not like Ana and
her visage that gave nothing away, confused people with

her lack of expression sometimes. When she wasn't being charming or sweet, that was, overcompensating without even knowing it.

'Let's go,' she slipped her arm through Solange's, unaware she was going to do that. Thinking some people just had it when it came to film, were transformed by the process. While others, beautiful women, stunning young men, couldn't make the transition. Were let down by the medium. She'd seen it happen again and again, bringing out the harshest of features in otherwise pretty faces, while making nondescript people glow, virtually glisten with life.

'Do you like our trees?' Ana's thoughts were interrupted by Solange. She followed the tilt of her chin to a tree which seemed to spread way out halfway up and crown itself in branches that ended in small green leaves. Her eyes moved from there to the small whitewashed house where they were staying. 'This one is called an *imbondeiro*,' Solange went on. 'You see them everywhere here.'

Ana nodded, thinking it was true, she had. Both in Luanda and down in Cabo Ledo, then in some of the paintings she and Solange had looked at in the outdoor market on the way back. She could still see the white one with the big brown tree at its centre, a gaggle of children and elders sitting around its trunk. She looked at Solange again, noticed how she was staring at the tree and suddenly felt herself go, drifting along on the movement of her mother's breath; rising, falling, hoping the moment would be prolonged before she pulled herself together.

'I remember this Mussulo when I was a girl and everything used to grow here. This island was so wild, so fertile,' Solange shook her head as they set off again. 'A lot of the plants have disappeared now. It's all this development, this building. Have you seen the other end of the island?' Ana nodded. 'Houses all thrown up one on top of another. It's like a concrete jungle. Wasn't like that when I was younger.'

'You came here with your family?' Ana wondered.

'Oh yes, yes,' Solange confirmed. 'Such a relief from the city; so wide open, so much space to play. I've always loved nature. Used to go camping with the girl guides all around the country when I was younger.'

'You were with the girl guides?' Ana grinned.

'*Sim*, senhora, all the girls in my family were with the guides. My father's idea, you know. He thought it would keep us out of trouble.'

Some chance, Ana thought as she heard Solange laugh. 'Didn't really work though did it?' the older woman spoke. 'And you, were you ever in the guides or anything like that, Ana?' she wanted to know.

'No, no, no,' Ana shook her head, thinking how she'd bristled as a teenager at anything that involved teamwork. Before she remembered that wasn't entirely true and told Solange how she'd acted in a couple of plays at the theatre in St Julian's, had even been convinced to do the costumes for *Macbeth* during her final year.

'I used to play volleyball as well, when I was a kid,' she added, 'ages ago.'

'Oh yes?' Solange smiled. 'We played basketball, my sisters and I. I was pretty good. Not as good as Ruth, you know.' Solange whistled. 'She was like a star, that one. Should have turned professional, gone and trained in the States but… Oh, well.'

'And do you still play?' Ana wondered, not really seeing Solange shooting hoops of an evening, finding it odd to imagine her as a teenage girl, gawky and shy as hell, jumping up into the sky.

'Yes, yes of course I do,' she replied. 'I mean not on a team or anything but I play with the girls at the orphanage, you know where I took you. And Oscar and I fool around on a court sometimes.'

'Is that right?' Ana could scarcely believe it.

'Yes, yes, he loves doing stuff like that. It's one of the reasons I like him, you know. He's so full of energy, always up to something. Like a child, gets so easily excited by the simple things in life.'

'That's nice, no?' Ana agreed.

'Oh yes,' Solange nodded. 'A lot of men here are just interested in material things now, things that aren't really important. Working, working like crazy, and all for what? No time with their wives, their families. No time to relax, just on and on. Next job, next job. That's no way to live! But Oscar, he's completely the opposite. So chilled out, doesn't let anything bother him. Says life's too short for all of that. I suppose he's good for me, really good for me. I can be a bit of a workaholic myself sometimes. What do you do, eh, to relax where you live, in Dublin?' she turned to look at Ana.

'I go to the cinema a lot,' Ana blurted out, then wondered if this could be filed under relaxation at all. Whether it was actually work, pleasure, or somewhere between the two. Scheduling films into her week before anything else. Before Conor even, when they were together, it was true. Though she'd never really owned up to doing that, had always tried to rationalise why it was she was watching five DVDs on a Sunday in November and not going for a walk in the park with him, or for a drink, or brunch. Sitting in front of the projector she'd bought for watching films at home, thinking there was so much she had to do the following week. And she could still remember that thought she'd had one after-noon, just as they were pulling away from one another, that at least she'd have more time now, more time to spend at the cinema on her own.

'I like swimming. I go to the pool sometimes,' she added. 'You know Guinness, the drink?'

Solange nodded her head, 'Yes, I've tasted it, but you know, I don't really drink much. It's very heavy, no?'

'Yes,' Ana agreed, smiling. 'Anyway, the brewery is close to where I live in Dublin.' She thought of enormous silver cylinders and the smoke coming from the plant seen from the other side of the river. And that afternoon in June when it had taken her by surprise, like a 1960s vision of what the future might look like. A possible scene from a parallel version of *A Clockwork Orange*. 'There's a swimming pool there, in the complex, a gym as well,' she came back to what she wanted to say. 'I go there sometimes.'

Ana saw the tiled mosaics on the walls, the tiered rows of benches for spectators, and remembered suddenly the reflection of the rectangular windows on the tiles beneath the Technicolor blue of the water. And that tingle of delight along her thigh at how the image appeared, disappeared, like a cinema screen, as the winter sun came out, went back in. God, there's no getting away from it, is there, she thought to herself, from film; from this obsessive fascination with the moving image?

'Look at them,' Solange interrupted her thoughts again, indicating a group of local boys diving from a concrete ramp into the sea.

'Wow!' Ana shook her head, watching a skinny frame somersault backwards into the air.

'*Bravo, bravo!*' Solange called as they passed, the kids turning around, one of them wolf-whistling after them, Ana laughing out loud before she noticed a wooden house just ahead.

She lifted her sunglasses and saw it was painted the mint green she had expected. 'It's Rui and Joana's house, Tiago's friends. I stayed there a couple of weeks ago, when we came to Mussulo. I don't believe it.' She thought of Lisete, wondered if she was there, then noticed as they got closer that the place seemed to have been locked up, the hammocks put away, the sand cleared of deckchairs.

But there was a shadow, a shadow by the door. Ana squinted, made out the figure of a bare-chested man standing on the veranda, looking out at the water. So still, so silent. It took her only a moment to recognise him as the local who'd helped them unload their food and luggage from the boat that day, who'd later grilled the fish he'd caught on the barbecue. Ana waved towards him. 'Everything good?' she called out.

'Everything good,' he confirmed. 'And you?'

'I'm good,' she replied as they walked up to him.

'And so you've returned?' he said as they stopped before him. 'Rui and the others are in Luanda. Back at work.'

'I know. Tiago too,' Ana responded. 'This, this is Solange, my mother,' she indicated the other woman.

'Solange, your mother? You two look like sisters,' he laughed, then kissed her on both cheeks. 'I'm Joaquim.'

'Ah yes, I've seen you before. I'm a friend of Bina's. She has the house down that way. The white house with the thatched roof.'

'Yes, yes,' Joaquim nodded. 'Bina, she was here at the weekend. In Luanda now as well, no?'

'Yes,' Solange responded. 'We're just here for the night.'

Ana looked at the man's chest as his eyes were on Solange, let her own irises travel the length of his torso, linger on the muscles around his big belly button. Wondering what he'd look like naked, underneath her. Before snapping out of it and turning her attention back to Solange, just as she was saying it had been nice to see him again, that they were going to walk to the other side of the island. 'Bye bye,' Ana couldn't help but give him a shot of a seductive smile as they left.

'You want to walk over that way, Ana, right? To the other side?' Solange looked for Ana to give her the go-ahead.

'Yes, of course,' she replied, remembering what Tiago had told her, how the waves were too strong to swim safely over there, out in the open ocean. She felt a rush of a certain wildness as they walked past Rui's house, like she was in the middle of a childish adventure again. Knowing, knowing of course, that there was no real danger or recklessness in their stroll, but excited nonetheless.

As they walked on past a group of cement shacks, the ground turned from flat sand to ridges that were more difficult to walk along and Solange paused for a moment, looked down. 'Must have got blown down in a storm,' she said, leaning over to inspect the trunk of an enormous palm tree lying on its side. 'The wind can get really strong here, very powerful, you know. It's so sweet in the *cacimbo*, when you're inside with something warm to drink and you can hear it rushing through the trees outside. It's beautiful, really beautiful…'

And that was the image that stayed with Ana for the rest of the walk, as they slowly made their way through the afternoon heat to the deserted beaches on the opposite side. Past another fallen tree and an abandoned wooden boat with all its metal rusted. That image of Solange behind a window, inside a house, looking at the movement of a season in the sand along the beach.

Luanda: July 1975

THE CONVERSATION. The confrontation. Set against the white walls of the sitting room: stark, clean, punishing. The room so solid against the weight of his words. Though they cannot be heard, the words. None of what José says, what Helena replies, is audible. All that can be witnessed is how they move, like dancers, from sofa to bookshelves to windows. Heads in hands, a book thrown in his direction, then another, then another, the only time any feeling registers on his face. Which is blank, frozen, most of those long hours as they pass their future back and forth to one another, like a ball, a bomb, watching as different possibilities unfold.

And these shots, these shots from home are intercut with something else, with another moving image. A close-up of a young woman sitting on a train, bound for Lubango, Sá da Bandeira as it was called then. Solange. Going in the opposite direction to the thousands of whites making their way to the capital, all their goods packed into vehicles, desperate to find a way out before the blacks take over in November. Solange is entirely silent too, mind twisting, trying to understand that life has brought her to this so early, that she has really got caught out so easily.

Back and forth, back and forth, from one scene to the other, as José and Helena sit across the table from one another now, as the train ploughs on through the country. Though still nothing can be heard, still it will be left to the young to try and put that conversation together, played over again and again over the years to come.

26

Luanda: January 2007

SHE'D BE GETTING READY NOW, wouldn't she, Solange? Rubbing moisturiser into her arms, sitting in front of the mirror, dusting some blusher onto her cheeks. Almost time to slip into her long pink dress with the flowers and leaves spilling down its front, which would flow as she walked out onto the stage.

Solange, where she should have been, by rights, thirty years earlier. Cheated of her chances. Commanding this stage in Angola only after she'd begun to make it in Europe. 'Like the old times, she's like a singer from the old days,' they'd say as she stood up by the microphone and grooved to the beat, lifting her arms up, throwing her head back, ensuring the clasping couples kept moving round the sandy ground.

But Ana wouldn't see any of this. Was staring, instead, over the runway of the airport. Sitting in the late afternoon sun of the restaurant terrace, smoking, drinking a glass of white wine and waiting for her food. Running her pearls through her long fingers, looking at her outfit reflected in other people's faces: the grey silk blouse, the man-tailored gabardine slacks, the black and cream Oxford shoes. She brushed her hair off her shoulders, pinned up at the front, curls falling down her back.

It's still very warm, isn't it?, she thought, watching the heat rise from the runway, wondering how cold it would be in Lisbon. She fanned her face with her book as the waiter brought her plate. Just a sandwich with French fries, wasn't all that sure of the food here, thought it better to be careful. '*Obrigada*,' she put out her cigarette, pushed the ashtray away and realised she was beginning to feel more at ease now, more confident, sure of herself. Because at first it had been a shock, hadn't it? Finding herself so entirely alone this afternoon, a bit daunting to stray back into the world, even if she'd thought she was ready for it. But, well, now she was beginning to look forward to the weekend in Lisbon: to some more of her own space, to being able to walk the streets without any worries. And to the new year in Dublin, all that lay ahead of her.

But back as well, she'd started looking over her shoulder also, it was true. At the four weeks that had passed in Luanda: the beaches of Mussulo, her days and nights with Solange, and the surreal nature of the city, which she'd come to see slowly as a place, a space, reconfigured, re-Africanised; not simply just a corpse of a colonial city.

She kept thinking about last night also, the night before. The dinner Solange had prepared in honour of her departure, having finally broken the news to the rest of her family about the daughter she'd had all those years ago. Ana remembered the surprise and the confusion of meeting her grandmother who sat across the table in a pretty green dress and smiled a lot, ran a time-worn hand across Ana's cheek as she was leaving.

Hours after Solange's sitting room had slowly, steadily,

begun to accumulate guests: first Tiago, Cristina, Ana and the girls, then Josefa, her husband and their grown-up son. Before Ruth, smiling, open-faced Ruth, not as intimidating as Ana had been led to believe, arrived with her dark, dark-skinned husband, busy helping his wife's mother by the arm. After the old woman's grandchildren, no, must be great-grandchildren, had tumbled in. With Oscar, of course, keeping it all going; filling up drinks, putting on music, and laughing, laughing heartily.

Leaving Ana to smile, to drink, barely able to move at the beginning, too self-conscious to throw her words into the clamour of voices occupying the room. Seizing her chance only when she saw Tiago move out to the balcony to have a cigarette. Filling up herself then because she could see the tears in his eyes at the thought that she was really leaving.

How strange to think all of that: last night, these past weeks, were turning into clearly defined memories now, Ana thought. That the process had begun almost as soon as she'd dropped off her bags and mounted the heavy marble steps that led up to the restaurant, the bar in the airport. Time moving in her stride and already pulling everything backwards, into a story, some kind of narrative.

She lit another cigarette and moved her plate away, looking down at the runway. Thinking of something Solange had said on that drive back from Cabo Ledo. How José had suggested leaving Helena once, so that he and Solange might start over together. And how she had refused, told him no out straight. Because she didn't want to settle down with an older married man, that wasn't what she wanted. And because she knew, when she saw them together, José and Helena, that they belonged together. That two people couldn't have loved one another more.

Luanda: November 1976

THEY SIT AROUND THE DINNER TABLE: José, Helena, Tiago and Ana, on a Thursday evening. A family, a form of a family. Over a year together already. Pretending that everything is fine, trying to carry on as normal, even though most of the city has emptied, most of their friends have gone.

With José beginning to look his age, older than his years perhaps, a hint of grey at the temples. Thinking still about what would have happened if he'd left Helena for Solange. If Helena had allowed him to go, if Solange had wanted him. He looks over at Ana, in Tiago's highchair, seeing her mother, seeing himself. It still catches him off guard sometimes, the fact he's ended up here, that this is how they live, that this is all there is. But he wonders if he would have felt any different if he was with Solange. Guesses he would have just been like David Bowie, haunted by memories of his family on their parched planet. How he's fallen to earth, José! How she's brought him to earth, Helena!

Helena, who looks tired, it's true, but still young, still pretty. Teaching, finally educating, the children of the *musseques*, up in Rangel. Or trying to, the most brazen of the boys just treating her with contempt; '*Angola é nossa!*

Angola is ours!' Yes, she thinks, but what now? What now for Angola, tumbling further into civil war? Oh, sometimes she curses herself for not forcing José to leave all those years ago, but mostly she knows there's no point. That it's better just to get on with things, that's what everybody has to do. At least she's locked her clown of a husband's box of tricks up for a while. Though she wonders, now and then, if she's doing the right thing by bringing up Ana. Is terrified every time Solange comes to visit that she'll take her baby girl for good. 'A minha filha é linda.'

Helena looks at Tiago. Tiago who is as contented and as easy-going as ever. Though sometimes, even if he hates to admit it, he's terrified at night. Falls into nightmares, dreaming of sharks holding onto his leg, pulling him underwater, out into the ocean, with none of his friends on the beach to see what is happening, nobody to call out to for help.

Tiago turns to Ana as she clatters her spoon down on the old highchair he gave to her. And smiles at her, thinking his mother and father don't think he knows where she came from, but he does, he knows all right. He wipes the baby's face with her bib, and asks his mother if he can hold her. Then takes her out, up, and into his arms, thinking they'll stick together, that's what they'll do, him and his little sister.

While Ana, Ana who so often seems so serious, so solemn, is nothing but smiles, smiles for her big brother tonight.

27

Lisbon: January 2007

SATURDAY MORNING AND THE TRAIN to Carcavelos. Ana was sitting with her cases before her, watching the river, looking blankly at the Christ the King statue on the opposite bank, the restaurants and bars of Alcântara, the monument to Portugal's explorers at Belém. Thinking of her father at home, waiting for her, because she refused to drag him all the way to the airport to pick her up. Deciding instead to make her own way out, to ring the buzzer and walk the flights of stairs. Take him in her arms and maybe, maybe after a few hours of coffee, of cake, tell him she'd found her, that she'd unearthed Solange.

She looked at the faded blue upholstery of the seats before her, traces of the sunlight of summers gone, then out the window again. And was startled, as usual, by the sudden expanse of water where the river meets the sea, before she began wondering if Solange would really come to Dublin later that year like she'd promised. And if, if she came, whether they'd take the DART to Dalkey and walk all the way to Killiney together. Down past Coliemore Harbour, along Sorrento Terrace and up onto Vico Road in the sunshine, the soft green mountains to the south and the sea to their left.

But for now though, she reminded herself again, she had her father to think about. Had to work out a plan of how she was going to broach the subject with him, tell him all she'd seen and heard, and ask him, yes, she had to ask him, for his side of the story. Request that he, please, for once and for all, tell her how it had all happened.

And yet as she noticed the boats bobbing in the January mist, she wondered if all of that couldn't wait. For the morning, at least, or the whole day. And whether they might, instead, not just spend the afternoon in the Atlântida Cine near their home; sitting together in the dark, as the lights went down, waiting for another film to begin.

Luanda: May 1977

A YOUNG FAMILY HURRIEDLY crossing the runway, walking up the steps and into the plane; José first, holding Tiago's hand, then Helena with Ana in her arms.

Helena, who turns as she gets to the top step, looking out over Luanda, over Angola. The image turns to a freeze-frame. Frame after frame after frame, as the strip of celluloid film slips out of the projector.

Acknowledgements

SPECIAL THANKS TO Adriana Ballester, Susan Kehoe Ferreira, Nuno Gonçalo Traguedo Ferreira, Luca and Luena Kehoe Ferreira, Esperança Emília da Silva Traguedo Ferreira, Marissa Moorman, Augusto Macola Vonga, Cristina Frawley, Sara Amido, Binha, Marionet, Lucas de Almeida, Hugo Miranda, Aniz Duran and Francisco Collazo.

I would like to acknowledge the receipt of two Travel and Training awards from the Arts Council of Irleand, which enabled me to travel to Angola and Portugal during the writing of this novel.

I would also like to acknowledge the receipt of a bursary from the Arts Council of Ireland, which enabled me to finish this novel. Thanks especially to Sarah Bannan for her support and encouragement.

My sincere gratitude to all at Serpent's Tail, most especially Pete Ayrton, John Williams, Rebecca Gray, Anna-Marie Fitzgerald and Ruthie Petrie.

Thanks to Patrícia Alexandra Traguedo Ferreira, Gonçalo Traguedo Mendes, Lara Hermenegildo Ferrim, Bernardo Hermenegildo Silva, Tia São do Jango, Ricardo Alves, Paulo Alves, Ana Tulia Henriques Augusto, Paulo Sergio Henriques Augusto, Sonia Castro, Maria Ivone Constantino, Maria

Florinda Constantino Figueredo, Jacinto Paulo, Donna Ana Pedro, Carlos Traguedo, the Collazo family in Madrid, Isabel Soares de Albergaria, Fergus Power, João Pimentel, Dr. Sara Moreira and her colleagues at the Cinemateca Portuguesa, Simona Accattatis at the ICA in Lisbon, Maíra Coleho, Rui Viana Pereira, Catarina Gouveia, Mumtaz, Miguel Sermão, Gina Tocchetto, João Gonçalo da Silva, Lucy Bolton, Elizabeth Brennan, Kelly-Anne Byrne, Hector Castells, Fiona Handyside, Barbara Henkes, Emma Keogh, Cecilia La Cruz, Alicia McGivern, Thomas McGraw-Lewis, Blathnaid Ní Murchú, Traolach Ó Murchú, Charlotte O'Connor, Karen Rigg, Norberto Rivero Sanz, all of my colleagues at the National College of Art and Design in Dublin especially James Armstrong, Silvia Loeffler and Hilary O'Kelly, the library staff at NCAD especially Seamus Gilna, the students at NCAD, John and Robert at NCAD, Siobhán Purves, Rachel Dempsey, Sandra Cooney, Olga Blasco, Olga Davis, Declan Pollock, Ben Payne, Ciarán Johnston, Kevin Gleeson, the students at Dublin Adult Learning Centre, Jessica Farnan, Jean-Paul Barsoum, Donatienne Lefort, Fenanda Lage Champinhon, Francele Sbardelotto De Bona, Adriano dos Santos Reis, Suzanne Humphreys, Inma Pinto, Carmen Planas, Monica Rodriguez-sedano, Declan Meade, Veronica Brogan, Lisa Downing, Fergal Finnegan, Tania Harada, Regan Hutchins, Paul Long, Anthony McGuinness, Belinda McKeon, Alma McQuade, Nicola Rogers, Mary Stokes, Nascimento, Colin Murphy, Sinéad Murphy, Mary Molloy, James Nunn, Angus O'Riordan, Adam Papp, Steven Place, Anji Pratap, Sarah-Jane Redmond, Nicola Rogers, Paddy Kehoe, Mary Kehoe and all the Kehoe family.

Lastly, I wish to acknowledge the help and support I received from all of those who would prefer to remain anonymous.